"Luke, I—I'm sorry. Truly. I was just trying to..."

"Protect your mother," he finished bitterly. "Well, it's a pity you didn't think what results your charade might produce. Because no sooner had I started thinking of you as my father's mistress, than I started wanting you as my own. I was well on the slippery slide to hell long before you started crying and I took you in my arms. I'm in hell now, still wanting you so badly it's killing me. But it's not love driving me. It's lust. Pure animal lust. At least I know the difference. So what am I to do, Celia? You tell me. Walk away like I've been trying to do? Or take you to hell with me? You choose, darling. You choose."

Secret Passions

by
Miranda Lee

Desire changes everything!

Book One:
A Secret Vengeance
March (#2236)
The price of passion is...revenge

Book Two:
The Secret Love-Child
April (#2242)
The price of passion is...a baby

Miranda Lee

A SECRET VENGEANCE

Secret Passions

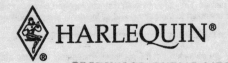

HARLEQUIN®

TORONTO • NEW YORK • LONDON
AMSTERDAM • PARIS • SYDNEY • HAMBURG
STOCKHOLM • ATHENS • TOKYO • MILAN • MADRID
PRAGUE • WARSAW • BUDAPEST • AUCKLAND

ISBN 0-373-12236-5

A SECRET VENGEANCE

First North American Publication 2002.

Printed in U.S.A.

PROLOGUE

CELIA was still half asleep when the phone rang. Lifting one eyelid, she glanced at her bedside clock radio.

Ten past eight. Not all that early, she supposed, but it was Sunday. Celia liked to sleep in on a Sunday. Everyone who knew her well, *knew* she liked to sleep in on a Sunday.

Which meant whoever was ringing her at this ungodly hour must have a good reason for doing so.

"Probably Mum," Celia muttered as she threw back her duvet and reached for the receiver.

"Hello," she said.

"He's dead," came a woman's voice, sounding spaced out.

Celia sucked in sharply and sat up. It *was* her mother. And Celia didn't have to ask who *he* was.

There was only one *he* in her mother's life. Lionel Freeman. Sydney's most awarded architect. Fifty-four years old. Married, with one grown-up son, named Luke.

Celia's mother had been Lionel Freeman's mistress for more years than her daughter liked to think about.

"What...what happened?" Celia asked, her thoughts whirling.

"He's dead," her mother repeated like a stuck record.

Celia took a deep breath and tried not to panic. "Is Lionel there with you now?"

"What?"

"Did Lionel come to visit you at Pretty Point this weekend?" Celia was thinking heart attack or stroke. The idea that they might have been actually *doing it* at the time brought a degree of revulsion. But it had to be faced. That was why Lionel Freeman visited his mistress after all. To have sex. And plenty of it, no doubt.

"No. No, he was going to, but then he couldn't make it."

Celia was torn between relief and anger. Her mother had wasted nearly half of her life waiting for her married lover to show up.

Well, now her waiting for Lionel was over. For good. But at what price?

"It was on the radio."

"What was on the radio, Mum?"

"They said it wasn't his fault. The other driver was drunk."

Celia nodded. Sounded like an accident of some kind. A car crash. And Lionel Freeman had been killed.

There was little pity in her heart for the man, only for her mother, her poor deluded mother who'd sacrificed everything for the illicit moments she'd spent with him. She'd loved Lionel Freeman more than life itself.

Now he was dead, and his distraught mistress was all alone in the secret love nest where the selfish Lionel had installed her a few years back.

Celia was terrified that, once the reality of her beloved's death sank in, her mum might very well do something stupid. Celia wasn't going to let that happen. Her mother had wasted twenty years of her life on Lionel Freeman. Celia wasn't going to let him take her with him in death.

"Mum, go and make yourself a cup of tea," she said firmly. "And put plenty of sugar in it. I'll be with you very soon."

Celia lived not all that far away, in Swansea. She also drove a zappy little hatchback which could move when she wanted it to.

Celia reached Pretty Point in twenty-three minutes flat. A record, considering it usually took her over half an hour. Of course, there'd hardly been a car on the road. The Sunday day-trippers from Sydney didn't swarm up in their droves till the seriously warm weather arrived, and summer was still a couple of months off.

"Mum?" she called out as she knocked frantically on the locked back door. "Mum, where are you? Let me in."

No answer. Celia's chest tightened like a vice as she raced round to the front of the house which faced the lake. She began imagining all kinds of horror scenarios.

But there her mother was, sitting at a table on the deck which overlooked the lake. The rising sun was behind her, outlining her perfect profile and glinting on her softly curled red-gold hair. She was wearing a silky lemon robe, sashed tightly around her still tiny waist. From a distance, she looked very young and very beautiful.

And, thankfully, very alive.

Celia heaved a great sigh of relief and hurried up the wooden steps which led onto the deck.

Her mother glanced up at her, her usually expressive green eyes worryingly vacant. She'd made the cup of tea, as ordered, but it sat in front of her, untouched.

She was still in deep shock, Celia realised.

"Mum," she chided gently as she sat down opposite her. "You haven't drunk your tea."

"What?"

"Your tea..."

"Oh... Yes... The tea. I'm sorry. I made it but I forgot to drink it."

"So I see." Celia decided against making another. Far better to get her mother away from here as soon as possible to a place where someone could watch her twenty-four hours a day for a while.

As much as Celia would have liked that person to be herself, she had a clinic to run and appointments that she simply had to keep this coming week. And the next week too. Maybe, by the end of that week, she could clear her diary somewhat and have some time off.

Meanwhile, Aunt Helen would have to come to the party, whether she wanted to or not.

"Mum," she said firmly, "you do know you can't stay here, don't you? This place belonged to Lionel. No doubt he kept it a secret from his family, but there will be a deed somewhere. Sooner or later, someone will show up and if you're still here, questions will be asked. You always told me Lionel didn't want his wife and son to know about you, so..."

"She's dead too," her mother broke in. "His wife. Kath. In the accident. They were both killed instantly."

"Dear heaven. How dreadful." Celia sagged back against her chair. She'd often wished Lionel Freeman would go take a running jump from one of his tallest buildings, but she'd never wished any harm on his unfortunate wife.

Poor woman, Celia thought.

"Poor Luke," her mother choked out. "He's going to be shattered."

Celia frowned. She didn't often think of the son, especially nowadays. He was a grown man after all, and not living at home. But now that her mother had mentioned him, she did feel sorry for the man. How awful to lose both his parents so tragically, especially his mother. Still, there was nothing she could do for him. She had her own shattered mother to worry about.

Her mum suddenly looked up, her eyes troubled. "You're right," she said in panicky tones. "I can't stay here. Luke might come. Lionel would die if Luke found out about me."

Once she realised what she'd just said, her face paled and a strangled sob escaped her throat.

"I doubt Lionel's son would come here personally, Mum," Celia reassured her. "But even if he does, you won't be here. I'm taking you to stay at Aunt Helen's for a while till I can organise something more permanent for you."

Her mother shook her head from side to side, tears flooding her eyes. "No. No, I couldn't go there. Helen didn't approve of my relationship with Lionel. She hated him.''

Didn't we all? Celia thought ruefully.

But this was hardly the time to say so.

"She hated what he did to you, Mum," Celia said gently. "Which is another thing entirely. And the situation's changed now, isn't it?"

"But she never understood," her mother cried, the tears spilling over. "You didn't either, did you, Celia? You thought I was wicked. And a fool."

"I never thought you were wicked, Mum."

"But you thought me a fool. And maybe I was. But love makes fools of all of us."

Not me, Celia vowed privately. Never! When and if she fell in love, it wouldn't be with a man like Lionel Freeman.

"I know you think Lionel didn't really love me," her mother said brokenly. "But he did."

"If you say so, Mum," was all Celia could say to that.

"You don't believe me."

Celia neither denied, nor confirmed this truth.

"There are things you don't know…things I've never told you…"

"And please don't go telling me now, Mum," Celia begged. The last thing she wanted to listen to was all the lies Lionel had fed his mistress to excuse and explain his two decades of adultery. She'd refused to discuss Lionel with her mother for some years now.

Her mother sighed a long shuddering sigh and, as the air left her lungs, so, it seemed, did her spirit. Her shoulders sagged. Her eyes dulled. Perhaps it was only the sun going behind a cloud, but so did her hair.

Suddenly, the eternally youthful and sensual creature that Lionel Freeman had lusted after so obsessively faded to nothing but a shadow of her former self. Till a moment before, she could have passed for thirty. Now, she looked every second of her forty-two years. And more.

"You're right," she said with a weariness that worried Celia more than her earlier shocked state. "What does anything matter any more? He's dead. Lionel is dead. It's over."

Celia gazed anxiously at her mother. This was what she'd been afraid of, her thinking there was nothing left to live for without the man she adored.

People said she was just like her mother, and she was, in looks. But, there, any similarities ended.

Her mother was a romantic, Celia, a realist. Especially when it came to men. Impossible for her to be otherwise after twenty years of watching her mother being so ruthlessly used by Lionel Freeman.

Perversely, there'd been a time when Celia had thought Lionel was wonderful. He'd entered her life when she'd been six, a lonely, fatherless little girl. What lonely little six-year-old wouldn't have adored the handsome man who'd made her mummy so happy when he'd visited, and had brought such marvellous toys?

It hadn't been till Celia had reached puberty that she'd taken off her rose-coloured glasses where her mummy's friend had been concerned. Once she'd realised exactly what Lionel came to visit for, and that he made her mother cry much more than smile, Celia's love for him had turned to hate overnight.

Outraged as only a disillusioned and disgusted teenager was able, she'd confronted Lionel and had torn strips off him, appalled when her mother had then torn strips off her in return for being out of line. But, after that, the lovers had met elsewhere other than at her mother's flat. Celia's mum had still cried a lot in the dead of night, and a distraught Celia had vowed never to grow up and fall in love with any man who wasn't a genuine Mr Wonderful. Her dream man wouldn't be afraid of commitment and fatherhood. And he certainly wouldn't be already married to someone else, like Lionel. He would be decent and honest, brave and reliable, loyal and loving.

Oh, and of course he'd be terribly good-looking and a really good kisser. She'd been only thirteen when she'd conjured up this vision of masculine perfection, after all.

Celia hadn't found him yet. In fact, she was pretty sure her Mr Wonderful didn't exist. She'd had quite a few boyfriends since leaving school, but hadn't found a single one who didn't eventually disappoint her, both in bed and out.

Maybe she had impossibly high standards. Her girlfriends always said she did. Whatever, her relationships never worked out.

The last one had been a couple of months ago. He'd been a footballer she'd treated for a knee injury, and he had pursued her to death after his treatments had finished, telling her he was simply crazy about her, promising her the world if she would just go out with him.

She had in the end, because she'd actually found him very attractive. She liked tall, well-built men. He was also surprisingly intelligent and seemingly sincere. Naturally, she'd made him wait for sex. She never went to bed with a guy on a first date. Nor a second. Nor even a third. When she finally had, she'd wished she hadn't. For it had been such an anticlimax.

He'd seemed pretty satisfied, however, which was always the case with men, she'd found. They really weren't too worried about their girlfriends' lack of orgasms, provided the girlfriend was coming across. They always blamed the woman, never themselves. And they invariably promised things would get better.

Sometimes, if the guy was nice, Celia hung in there, hoping things *would* improve. But when the footballer had sensitively informed her during his second go that his previous girlfriend would have come three times by then, Celia had decided Mr Wonderful he wasn't. Nor ever would be.

She'd dumped him the next morning.

Pity her mother hadn't dumped Lionel Freeman the morning after all those years ago when she'd found out he was married. But then, Lionel, in bed at least, *had been* her mother's Mr Wonderful. Apparently, she did refuse to see him for a little while. But the manipulative devil had wormed his way back into her bed with all those excuses and lies Celia didn't want to hear about, and he'd been there on a regular basis ever since.

Celia didn't doubt it was a case of true love on her

mum's part, but she would put a million dollars on it being nothing but lust on darling Lionel's.

Celia wanted to be angry with her mother for being such a romantic fool all these years but, somehow, she couldn't. Not today. Not when the poor woman's heart was already breaking apart.

"Why don't you go shower and dress while I ring Aunt Helen?" she suggested gently.

Fortunately, Celia's aunt lived less than ten miles away, over at Dora Creek. Her husband, John, worked at the local power station. Their two sons had long grown up and left home, so they had plenty of spare bedrooms.

Her mother shrugged listlessly. "Whatever."

"We'll just pack you a small case of essentials for now. I can come back at a later date and get the rest of your things." There was no real hurry. Under the circumstances, Celia couldn't see anyone turning up here for ages. She doubted Lionel's son ever would personally. Seriously rich people had lackeys to attend to such matters. And Luke Freeman was now a seriously rich man.

She stood up, her car keys still in her hand.

Her mother levered herself up slowly before glancing around with sad eyes. "Lionel really loved this place," she said wanly. "He designed and built it, especially for us."

Celia didn't doubt it. The A-framed cabin with its glass façade and large wooden decks overlooking the lake made the perfect love nest. Remote and beautiful in setting, the open-plan interior was filled with all the romantic accoutrements lovers would appreciate. A huge sandstone fireplace, complete with deep squashy sofas flanking a plushly piled cream rug. Upstairs, the loft bedroom was dominated by a king-sized bed, with the adjoining bathroom sporting a spa bath which could easily accommodate two.

No guest room, of course. Lionel had never wanted his mistress to have guests.

Celia had never stayed here overnight. Neither did she drop in on a weekend, unless her mother gave her the all clear. Running into Lionel had been something to be avoided at all costs since she'd grown up, because Celia had known she would have been vicious to him if the occasion had arisen.

But she visited her mother at least once during most weeks. And regardless of the day, she always knew if Lionel had visited the previous weekend. He'd had this distinctive cologne that he'd always worn, and that had lingered long after he'd been gone. She could remember smelling it in her mother's bedroom as a child, especially when she'd climbed into her mother's bed in the morning. It always disturbed her to remember how much she'd liked the smell back then. And how much she'd liked Lionel.

"Mum, let's go," Celia said brusquely, and took her mother's arm.

Jessica went quietly, because she knew it was for the best. There were too many memories of Lionel at Pretty Point. Too many ghosts to haunt her at night. Too many bad thoughts waiting to assail her.

She'd always believed Lionel had genuinely loved her, that his passion for her had been more than sexual.

Now, Jessica wasn't so sure. Often, in the past, when she hadn't seen Lionel for some time, she'd begin having these terrible doubts. But once he'd arrived and had taken her in his arms again, all her doubts would vanish.

But he would never take her in his arms again. Never make love to her again. Never tell her how much she meant to him again.

Which meant her doubts would never be put to rest. They would fester and grow like some dreadful disease.

Jessica's heart seemed to disintegrate in her chest under the weight of this appalling prospect. For if she didn't believe Lionel had loved her as much as she'd loved him, then what had been the point of all the sacrifices she'd made? Never to write to him, nor send him cards. Never to spend Christmas or birthdays with him. Never to go anywhere in public with him.

Never to have his child.

Had it all been a waste of time? Had his love for her been a horrible illusion? Had he really been a deeply sensitive man...or a wickedly selfish liar?

She couldn't bear to think such thoughts. Couldn't bear it.

Suddenly, she began to sob, great heaving sobs which racked her whole body.

"Oh, Mum," her daughter cried and hugged her close. "You'll be all right. You'll see. We just have to get you away from here."

CHAPTER ONE

"IS THAT everything, Harvey?" Luke asked, putting his pen away in his jacket pocket and pushing the papers back across the desk.

"Yes. For now," the solicitor answered, stacking up all the forms and sliding them into a file.

Luke went to rise from his chair.

"No, wait. There is another small matter concerning your father's estate which I need your advice upon."

Luke sat back down and glanced at his watch. It was a quarter to one. He was to meet Isabel downstairs at one for lunch, after which they were going shopping for their wedding rings. "What is it?"

"The Friday before the accident, your father came to see me about a waterfront property he owned on Lake Macquarie."

Luke frowned. "You wouldn't be talking about a place on Pretty Point, would you?"

"Yes. That's the place. Pretty Point. It's a ten-acre holding, plus a single-bedroomed residence."

Luke's frown deepened. "I thought Dad had sold that old place years ago. He'd said he didn't use it any more because the fishing in the lake wasn't what it used to be."

His father had been mad about fishing. He'd taken Luke fishing with him as soon as he'd been old enough to hold a line. By the time Luke was six or seven, father and son would often go away for the weekend together, mostly to the cabin at Pretty Point which had a jetty and a small runabout moored there permanently. Luke's mother had always stayed home on these occasions. She'd hated everything to do with fish. The smell. The feel. Even the taste.

Luke had loved those weekends, but not because of the fishing. It was his dad's company and attention he'd loved. In all honesty, Luke found fishing about as fascinating as watching grass grow.

Luke's discovering basketball in a big way around twelve had finally forced him to confess that he didn't want to go away fishing any more. He'd wanted to spend his weekends at the local youth club, practising his basketball skills and competing in tournaments.

His dad had been very understanding, as he'd always been understanding. He'd been a great dad. And a great husband too.

Of course, his mum had been a wonderful wife as well, one of the old-fashioned kind who hadn't worked, and had devoted herself entirely to her husband and son, a woman who'd taken pride in keeping her home spotless and doing all the cooking and cleaning herself, even though they could well have afforded paid help.

Yet she hadn't been the strongest of women, healthwise, suffering from terrible migraines. Luke could remember as a boy having to be extra quiet around the house when she was having one of her attacks. His father would often come home from work to sit with his wife in her darkened bedroom.

Such a devoted couple.

And now they were both dead, victims of some stoned individual in a four-wheel drive who'd crossed over to the wrong side of the road and had collected his dad's car, head on.

Come tomorrow, the accident would have happened two weeks ago. It had been on a Saturday night, just this side of midnight. It had happened on the Mona Vale road. They'd been returning from a dinner party at Narrabeen.

They'd only been in their mid-fifties. Hardly old. Talk about life being unfair.

Luke shifted in his seat and cleared his throat. What had Harvey been asking him? Oh, yes...about the week-ender at Pretty Point.

"I guess Dad didn't get round to selling the old place after all," he said. "He could be sentimental at times. So what did he want to do with it?"

"He wanted to gift it over to a lady friend of his."

Luke was taken aback. "*Who*?" he demanded to know.

"A Ms Jessica Gilbert."

Luke frowned. Who on earth was Ms Jessica Gilbert?

"I don't recognise the name," he ground out, trying not to think the impossible, but thinking it all the same.

"Don't jump to conclusions, Luke," Harvey advised. "You and I both know your father wasn't that kind of man."

Luke certainly hadn't thought so. Till now. He'd hero-worshipped his father, and had always wanted to be just like him, in every way.

"Did Dad tell you anything about this Ms Gilbert?" he asked, his gut tightening.

"Not all that much. He said she was a lovely lady, to whom life hadn't been very kind, and whom he wanted to help. Apparently, she doesn't own a home of her own and he'd been letting her live in the place at Pretty Point for the last few years, rent free. He thought it best if he gifted the property over to her and then she'd have a secure roof over her head for life."

Luke's inner tension began to ease. His father was well-known for his charitable gestures. But, for a moment there...

"Your father was worried that if he died suddenly and the present rent-free arrangement came to light, your mother might do exactly what you just did: jump to all the wrong conclusions."

"I feel terrible for thinking the worst," Luke confessed, "even for a moment."

"Don't be too hard on yourself. I had a few doubts myself when Lionel first told me, especially when he asked me to be very discreet and not mention it to a soul. But I only had to think of how totally devoted he was to your mother to know I couldn't be more wrong. So, shall I go ahead then," Harvey asked, "and gift the property over to this Ms Gilbert?"

"Yes, yes, draw up the necessary papers and I'll come back and sign them when they're ready."

"I thought you'd say that. Your father would be proud of you, Luke. After all, waterfront properties of that size on Lake Macquarie, regardless of how remote, are worth a bundle these days."

"I'm only doing what Dad wanted. And it's not as though I haven't inherited enough property." As well as the family home in St Ives, Luke now owned several investment units all over Sydney, some right in the CBD. It seemed every time his father had designed a large block of units, part of his fee had been to keep one of them.

"I must go, Harvey," Luke said. "I'm meeting Isabel downstairs at one."

"Ah. The lovely Isabel. What a glorious bride she's going to make. It's such a tragedy to have this dreadful thing happen so close to your marriage."

"Yes. I was going to postpone the ceremony, but things are a bit too far along for that. Isabel's parents have already spent a small fortune, and they're not wealthy people."

"Your own parents wouldn't have wanted you to postpone a single thing, Luke. Your father was especially delighted you were settling down to family life here in Australia. He missed you a lot when you went overseas to work. He was worried you might marry some foreign girl and never come back."

"He should have known I would never do that," Luke said swiftly, and stood up. "I'll see you and your wife at the wedding, then?"

Harvey stood up as well. "Looking forward to it."

Both men shook hands across the desk and Luke left, grateful to have at least temporarily finished with the legal and practical problems that had followed his parents' deaths. There'd been so much to do, so many arrangements, so many decisions to be made. Too many, really.

But being an only child, there'd been no one else. The buck stopped with him.

He hoped he'd done everything well, and properly. He hoped his father *was* proud of him.

Luke's mind returned to Ms Jessica Gilbert on the ride down in the lift and he wondered who she was and how his father had come to know her. Had she been an ex-employee? A loyal secretary who'd worked for him during his early days as a struggling architect? Maybe the cleaning lady who'd looked after the place at Pretty Point all those years ago? Luke recalled some local woman had come in to clean up after them.

Or was she some poor unfortunate whose hard-luck story had come to his dad's attention through one of the various charities he'd given money to? Some elderly spinster who'd never had much, and never would.

Luke thought this last scenario a likely one. His father liked to help little old ladies.

Even so, it was only a guess. He wished Harvey had known more. It was irritating, not knowing the full circumstances behind such a substantial bequest. The weekender at Pretty Point, though small and a bit ramshackle, *was* sitting on a parcel of valuable land.

Maybe, when the time came, he'd take the gifted deed up to the woman personally. That way his curiosity would be well and truly satisfied, and this tiny but nagging doubt that his father might not have been so perfect after all would be safely banished.

Luke still hadn't made up his mind on the issue when

the lift doors opened and there, straight ahead, stood Isabel, looking classy and coolly beautiful, as usual. She was wearing a simple black dress and her long blonde hair was sleekly up, showing off her elegant neck, and the diamond earrings he'd given her recently for her birthday.

She smiled at him, one of those serene smiles that had a soothing effect on Luke, no matter how stressed out he was. He smiled back as he walked towards her, thinking how lucky he was to have found a woman like Isabel to marry. Not only beautiful, but so sensible and level-headed.

He never had to put up with jealous scenes or possessive demands with her as he had with previous girlfriends. On top of that, Isabel could cook like a cordon bleu chef and actually considered being a wife and mother a career in itself. Just like his mum.

She'd already quit her job as receptionist at the large architectural firm Luke was currently contracted to and where they'd met at last year's Christmas party. She had no plans to go back to work after their marriage. They were going to start trying for a baby straight away.

Of course, Isabel *was* thirty, with a whole lifetime of experiences behind her, so she was ripe and ready for settling down, as Luke was himself at thirty-two. Like him, she'd travelled extensively, *and* admitted to several lovers, something that didn't bother Luke one little bit.

He liked the fact Isabel was experienced in bed. He liked it that she wasn't insecure with him. He especially liked the fact she wanted the same things he wanted: a marriage that would last, and a family of at least two children.

Okay, so he wasn't in love with her, and vice versa. But darn it all, he'd fallen in love a few times in the past, and he hadn't really liked the feel of it. It wasn't stable for starters. And it never lasted.

By the time Luke had decided it was time to settle down, he'd concluded romantic love was not a sound basis for marriage. Isabel had reached the same conclusion after a few disastrous love affairs of her own.

Which meant they were perfectly in tune with each other. They had the same goals, and they never ever argued, which was something Luke valued very highly.

Arguments and disagreements always upset him. Quite a lot. He wanted none of that in his marriage. He wanted peace, and harmony. He wanted what his father had had with his mother.

"All finished?" Isabel asked, reaching up to kiss him on the cheek.

"For the time being," he returned, his thoughts sliding once again back to the mysterious Ms Gilbert. Frustrating, really. Why couldn't he forget about her? He opened his mouth to tell Isabel about the woman, then he closed it again. Why, he wasn't sure. Perhaps because he didn't want to see that awful doubt about his father in *her* eyes as well.

Ms Gilbert was just a charity case, Luke reassured himself, some poor little old lady who didn't have the wherewithal to help herself. To think anything else was untenable.

But the more Luke tried to picture Ms Jessica Gilbert

as some poor little old lady, the less he was convinced. His father wouldn't have been worried about his mother jumping to the wrong conclusions if the woman was elderly. He would only have worried about jealousy if the woman was young. And attractive.

"Is there something wrong, Luke?"

"Would you mind very much if I took a rain check on lunch, plus the ring-buying expedition?" he said on the spur of the moment. "There's something I simply must do which can't wait."

"What, for heaven's sake?" She wasn't angry, just puzzled.

"I need to drive up to Lake Macquarie."

Isabel blinked her surprise. "Lake Macquarie! But *why*?"

Why, indeed?

"There's a property up there, an old fishing cabin where Dad used to take me when I was a boy. I haven't been there for years. I just found out that he didn't sell it like I thought he had. I know it sounds crazy but I have this compulsion to see it again."

"And you have to go see it this very day, this very afternoon?"

"Yes."

He expected her to ask more questions but she just smiled a wry smile. "You're a lot more sentimental than you think you are, Luke Freeman. Look, why don't you drive up there and stay the weekend? Have a rest. It'll do you the world of good. These last two weeks must have been dreadful for you."

Yes, he *could* stay the night at least, if he wanted to.

He knew where his father had always hidden the key and he doubted that would have changed.

"You wouldn't mind?" he said.

Isabel shrugged. "Why should I mind? In just over two weeks' time, I'll have you for the rest of my life. I think I can spare you for a couple of days' R and R. But, Luke, I don't want to put off buying the rings. They might need to be resized. Would you trust me to choose them without you?"

Luke couldn't think of any other female he'd ever known who was so blessedly lacking in being a drama queen about things. "You are one incredible woman, do you know that? Here. Take this credit card and put the rings on that. And put lunch on it too."

"If you insist," she said, smiling saucily as she whipped the card out of his fingers.

"I insist," he said, and smiled warmly back at her.

Another thing about Isabel that Luke appreciated was the fact she didn't pretend she didn't like money. She did. Even before the tragedy, which had turned him into a multimillionaire overnight, Isabel had openly appreciated the fact that he was earning a high six-figure salary, owned a town house in Turramurra, drove a recent-model BMW, and could afford to take her to Dream Island on their honeymoon.

Now, of course, he could afford a whole lot more.

"I'll call you later," he promised.

"You'd better."

"And you're right. I might stay up there for a day or two." Depending on what he found once he got there, of course.

"I've already told you to."

"I'll miss you," he said, and kissed her on the cheek.

"You call that a kiss?"

He laughed, then kissed her on the mouth. Her tongue touched his and Luke momentarily regretted not making love with Isabel the night before. But, at the time, he hadn't wanted to. He hadn't wanted sex in any way, shape or form since the funerals.

"Mmm." His lips lifted and he smiled wryly down at her. "I might come back tonight after all."

"Waste of time, handsome. I'm taking Rachel out to dinner and the theatre tonight, remember? I can't put it off. I've already arranged everything."

"I wouldn't want you to put it off," he told her. Rachel was an old school friend of Isabel's from her boarding school days. She'd once been a top secretary at the Australian Broadcasting Corporation, but she hadn't worked for some years. Nowadays, she spent twenty-four hours a day, seven days a week, looking after her foster mother who had Alzheimer's.

Luke could well imagine how much Rachel looked forward to the one night a month off Isabel organised for her. He'd met her once briefly, and had thought how tired and old she'd looked. Yet she was only a year older than Isabel.

"It'll keep, won't it?" Isabel added.

"Sure." Luke shrugged, the need already fading. They'd never gone through one of those lust-driven stages where they'd just had to have each other, regardless of where they were, or what was going on around them. They'd become friends before they'd become lovers. Some engaged couples Luke knew couldn't keep their hands off each other, even in public. He and Isabel were never like that.

Which perhaps explained why his father had taken Luke aside at his engagement party and had questioned him on whether he was completely happy with Isabel in bed. Luke had been taken aback at the time by his father's grilling over their sex life, but he had assured him that everything was fine in the bedroom department.

Thinking of this instance, however, suddenly made Luke wonder if his father had been totally happy with *his* sex life. To all intents and purposes, Luke's parents had *seemed* happy with each other. They were openly affectionate with each other. Always holding hands and hugging. But who knew what happened behind closed doors?

Luke imagined that a man dissatisfied with his sex life might be tempted to stray...

"I think you'd better get going, Luke," Isabel said drily. "You've drifted off somewhere again."

"Sorry."

"You were thinking of your father, weren't you?"

Luke stared at her.

"You don't have to look at me like that. I know what he meant to you. And I know how much you'll miss him. Much more than your mother. Oh, I know you loved your mother too. How could you not? She was the nicest, sweetest lady. But your father was more to you than a parent. He was your best friend. And your hero. So go and talk to him for a while up at that old place on Lake Macquarie. He'll be there, I'm sure. And he'll listen to you, as he always did.''

Luke now wished he'd told Isabel the complete truth about Pretty Point. He hadn't realised she had such sensitivity. She always seemed so pragmatic about things.

But it was too late now. She'd wonder why he hadn't been honest with her right from the start. And their relationship might suffer.

But it was a valuable lesson learned. He vowed to always tell his fiancée the truth in future, no matter what.

CHAPTER TWO

WHEN the idea to go to Pretty Point for the weekend first popped into Celia's head, she'd immediately rejected it. But the more she'd thought about it, the more she'd realised that Lionel's love nest was the perfect getaway.

And, brother, did she need to get away.

The last two weeks had left her totally and utterly drained. She'd spent every evening and all the previous weekend over at Aunt Helen's, either sitting with her almost catatonic mother, or arguing with her aunt over what should be done about her.

Celia wanted her mother to see a psychiatrist, and to get onto some medication for depression, but her sister disagreed.

"Jessica isn't crazy," Helen had stated firmly last night. "Just broken-hearted. All she needs is time, and some tender loving care and she'll come good. You'll be the one needing medication shortly if you keep worrying about her the way you are. Now, I don't want to see hide nor hair of you this weekend, Celia. Go out with your friends. Or better still, go away somewhere. *Anywhere.*"

Celia lent back in the deck chair with a sigh and thought *anywhere* had never looked so good. What was it about a water view that relaxed nerves and soothed even the weariest soul?

She had to give to Lionel. He'd built his love nest on one superb spot.

He'd also had great taste in wine.

Celia took another sip of the excellent Chablis she'd found chilling in the fridge door and thought how lucky it was that her last appointment had cancelled that afternoon. She always tried to finish up early on a Friday but it was a real stroke of luck to finish at lunch-time. By two o'clock, she'd been packed and on her way to Pretty Point, with only a small detour necessary for some groceries.

And now here she was, mid-afternoon, with a lovely glass of wine in her hands, a million-dollar view to enjoy, and two days of blissful peace and solitude to look forward.

Celia kept on sipping the wine and gradually, the tension melted out of her knotted neck and shoulder muscles till she was leaning back, feeling deliciously mellow. Alcohol, she decided, was proving much more relaxing than all the head rotating exercises she'd been trying on herself every night this week. And infinitely more relaxing than Joanne's solution.

"What you need, honey," Celia's fellow physio at the clinic had said yesterday, "is to get laid."

Pig's ear, she did.

Sex never relaxed Celia. Her only feelings afterwards were disappointment, disillusionment and dismay.

But that was just her, she'd finally accepted. Sex *was* widely accepted as a very pleasurable activity, as well as being touted as mother nature's sleeping pill. *She* was the abnormal one.

Her mother had obviously been very partial to sex. With Lionel, anyway.

More than partial. She'd been possessed by it.

Celia wondered what it would be like to experience the sort of uncontrollable passion that turned an otherwise intelligent, independent woman into some kind of mindless sex slave. Had the pleasure of the moments spent with Lionel compensated for her mother's pain afterwards? Had a weekend of sex and excitement with him been worth weeks of subsequent depression?

Celia had to assume her mother thought it had. Otherwise, why keep on doing it?

Maybe if *she* was ever swept up in a *grande* passion—or even a *petite* passion—Celia might understand her mother's masochistic behaviour. As it was, from an objective, outsider's point of view, such an all-consuming passion seemed nothing better than a slow-acting poison. One of those corrosive substances that ate away at one's insides till there was nothing left but a dying shell.

Her mother had been well on the way to being reduced to such a shell long before Lionel had died. Hopefully, his death had come just in time and Aunt Helen was right: with a bit of tender loving care Celia's mother might not end up having a complete nervous breakdown, nor going stark raving mad.

On the other hand…

Celia scowled at herself. She really didn't want to

think about her mother's ill-fated relationship with Lionel Freeman this weekend.

Difficult not to, however, considering where she was. The place still reeked of the illicit lovers. Celia might have cleared all the rooms of her mother's things, but Jessica's highly individual decorating touch remained, as did loads of Lionel's personal possessions. Clothes. Stacks of CDs. Shelves full of books. And bottles and bottles of wine.

Celia sighed. It had been a mistake to come here. She'd been right to reject the idea when it had first occurred to her. What on earth had she been thinking of?

But she was stuck here for now. She'd had too much to drink on an empty stomach to drive anywhere at the moment. Maybe later on this evening, she would go home.

And maybe not.

The bitter truth was she'd end up thinking of her mother at the moment, no matter where she was. Might as well stay here, Celia decided wearily.

Might as well have another glass of wine, too.

Luke was lost. Hopelessly lost. He'd thought he knew the way. But it had been nearly twenty years since he'd been to Pretty Point and, even then, he'd only been a child passenger, not the adult driver.

The relatively new freeway showed no turn-offs to Pretty Point, nor to any other place names he recognised. He realised after sailing past the turn-off to Morisset and Cooranbong that he probably should have taken it. He'd been driving north way too long. Nearly two hours from Sydney. He took the next turn-off to Toronto, drove into the town and bought a local map at a newsagent's.

After studying it for a while, he made his way back onto the expressway, took the correct turn-off, and fifteen minutes later began to finally see some familiarity in the roads.

Even so, the area had changed dramatically.

Bush had been cleared and housing estates had popped up all over the place, even on Pretty Point. It was certainly no longer a backwater. As he drove down the now tarred road which led to the far end of the Point—and his father's property—Luke began to appreciate how much ten acres of waterfront land was worth here in the present climate.

Ms Jessica Gilbert, whoever she was, had done very well for herself out of his father's generosity.

Luke's tension grew as he drew closer, his eyes narrowing as he glimpsed a building through the trees, a triangular-shaped house with a sloping green roof. He slowed, then braked, then scratched his head. Had his memory played him false? The area looked right, but the house was all wrong.

He drove on slowly, looking for a sign that this was the right place. And there it was, on the big white gum tree with the gnarled branches. His childish message, carved into the trunk all those years ago. LF was here.

Luke's stomach contracted. The place was right. But the house was definitely wrong. He stared at it again.

It looked almost new, built on exactly the same spot where the old cabin had stood.

If his father had built a new weekender up here, then why hadn't he ever mentioned it to him?

Don't jump to conclusions, he warned himself. All will be explained once you meet its occupier in the flesh.

Meanwhile, Luke clung to the hope that the new place had originally been built as an investment property—possibly when he'd been living in England. Maybe his father had intended to sell it, but then had generously allowed this Ms Gilbert to live there, once he'd heard her hard-luck story.

Luke directed his car down the gravel driveway which wound a gentle path through the tall trees and up towards the back porch of the A-framed dwelling.

A sporty white hatchback was parked next to the steps.

Not a car that an elderly spinster would drive.

Luke tried not to keep jumping to a not-very-nice conclusion, but it was increasingly hard.

He climbed out from behind the wheel and rather reluctantly mounted the long back porch, all the while frowning down at the pine decking, then up at the pine logs which made up the entire back wall of the house.

One of his father's favourite woods had been pine.

Luke knew then that his father had not just had this place built, he'd designed it himself. Had designed and had built it without telling him. Without telling his wife as well, Luke warranted.

Clenching a fist, he rapped on the door. There was

no doorbell, of course. His father had hated doorbells. He'd hated phones as well. He'd hated anything that made irritating interrupting noises.

Luke knocked again. Louder this time.

Twenty more seconds ticked by. Twenty more silent tension-twisting seconds.

Why didn't the woman answer? Was she deaf?

Suddenly, Luke hoped she was just that. Deaf. Elderly people were often deaf.

The door was reefed open and she stood before him. In the flesh.

She wasn't old. *Nor deaf.*

She was young. And beautiful. With full lips, slanting green eyes and glorious red-gold hair.

It was up. But not like Isabel wore hers up, all neat and smooth and confined. This hair defied order, rebellious curls easily escaping their loose prison to kiss the skin on her slender neck and rest lightly against her smooth, pale-skinned face.

"Ms Gilbert?" he demanded to know, his voice curt, his stomach churning. Maybe it wasn't her. Maybe she was a friend. A welfare officer. A community nurse, even.

And maybe he was the next winner of the Nobel prize for architecture. If there was one.

"Yes," she admitted, and Luke finally knew the answers to every question he'd been asking himself since he'd first heard her name.

CHAPTER THREE

CELIA stared up at the dark haired and very handsome man standing in the doorway, her memory trying to place him. His face was familiar, and so were his eyes. Almost black, they were. Long lashed and very deeply set.

She was frowning into their inky depths when recognition struck.

"Dear heaven," she said, her hand tightening on the door knob. "You must be Luke. Lionel's son." She kept on staring at him. Impossible not to. It was like seeing Lionel, twenty years ago.

"Right in one, Ms Gilbert."

The fact that he knew *her* name took a moment or two to register. As did his simmering anger.

Clearly, Luke Freeman hadn't come to claim or inspect an inheritance. Somehow, he'd found out about his father's extramarital affair with her mother, and had come charging up here, far from happy.

But what did he want? To hear first hand all of the sordid details? To confront his father's mistress personally? To tear strips off her for corrupting his precious parent?

Over my dead body, Celia vowed. Her mother had suffered enough at the hands of one Freeman man. She wasn't about to let the son finish off what the father had started.

She crossed her arms and gathered herself to do battle. "I don't how you found out," she said through gritted teeth, "but I presume you know everything."

"About your affair with my father, you mean?" he returned in a voice that would have cut diamonds. "Oh, yes, I know. *Now.* But I suspected the truth as soon as you opened the door. To give my father credit, he had taste. You are one beautiful woman, Ms Jessica Gilbert."

Celia was too shocked to be even mildly flattered by this back-handed compliment. My goodness! He thought *she* was his father's mistress!

She opened her mouth to tear strips off *him*, but then slowly closed it again, her mind racing to put this puzzle together. If he thought *she* was his father's bit on the side, then he actually knew very little. Just a name. Not the woman in question's age. Nor anything else about her. He certainly had no idea Ms Jessica Gilbert was a forty-two-year-old single mother with a twenty-six-year-old daughter. He definitely had no idea how long the affair had been going on.

Celia could say anything she liked and Lionel's son would probably believe it.

She thought of her mother and knew what she had to do.

Celia sighed, uncrossed her arms and stepped back out of the doorway. "I suppose you'd better come in," she said with a wave of her hand, all the while wondering what approach she should take for the part of Lionel's secret mistress.

His son was no fool, so best stick to the truth as much as possible so that she didn't slip up. She would simply bring the affair forward twenty years and put herself in her mother's place.

It would be difficult to pretend she'd loved the ruthless Lionel, let alone made love with him.

But she'd manage.

Somehow.

Luke tried to get a grip on his anger as he accepted her reluctant invitation and stepped into his father's secret love nest.

He failed wretchedly. But who, exactly, was he angry with? His father, for not living up to his hero status? Or this creature, this incredibly sensual creature of the captivating and cat-like green eyes?

Luke strode across the large open-plan living room, his eyes taking in at a glance the simple yet elegant beauty of the place. The extensive use of wood had his father's hand stamped all over it, though not everything was made of pine inside, only the kitchen and the walls. The polished wooden floors were boxwood and the high panelled ceiling looked like various types of cedar. The dining room table was made in a rich walnut, the finely carved chairs fashioned in the same wood, with dark green velvet cushions. The huge sofa facing the sandstone fireplace was also covered in the same dark green velvet.

As Luke walked past it, he couldn't help thinking

about what might have transpired on that sofa between his father and his mistress. And on the plush-pile cream rug stretched out on the floor in front of the fireplace. He could see her red-gold hair now, spread out and glowing in the fire light. He could almost feel the warmth of the flames on her pale skin, and practically taste the siren sweetness of her lips, drawing her married lover down, down into the hell-fires where lust ruled and faithfulness was totally forgotten.

Luke wrenched out one of the dining chairs and plonked himself down sideways in it, one elbow on the table, his other on the back of the chair. No way was he going to sit on the sofa. Nor make himself too comfortable. This was going to be a very brief visit.

"Would you like a drink?" she asked politely after shutting the door. "Tea? Coffee? A glass of wine?"

"No, thanks." No politeness in *his* voice. It was rough and gruff.

"I think, perhaps," she murmured in her sweet siren's voice, "I could do with one."

He watched her walk over to the galley-style kitchen, his gaze sweeping down her body then up again.

She was mistress material all right, with curves in all the right places. And she dressed for the part. Long, floaty wraparound skirt in a deep burgundy colour. A black knitted cardigan top with a deep scooped neckline and easy-to-undo buttons. No bra. Bare feet.

Luke estimated it would take a man less than twenty seconds to strip her naked, if she made no objections.

The image of his father sweeping through that door and immediately doing just that brought a flood of fierce

feelings within Luke. More anger. A degree of disgust.
And a perturbing amount of jealousy!

She poured herself a glass of white wine from a bottle
in the fridge and came round to slide up on one of three
pine stools which faced the kitchen counter. But she
didn't face the kitchen counter. She faced him, her
green eyes thoughtful.

"What *do* you want, then?" she said as she crossed
her legs and lifted the glass to her lips.

When her skirt fell slightly apart to show more than
a tantalising glimpse of shapely leg, Luke struggled to
banish the X-rated images that zoomed into his mind.

"I just want to talk to you," he replied, pleased that
his tone was a bit more businesslike and less angry.

Her delicate eyebrows arched cynically, and Luke
wondered if his father had told her he only wanted to
talk to her when they'd first met.

The image of his father as a ruthless womaniser
didn't sit any better with Luke than the image of him
as a seduced fool.

He'd thought he'd known all the answers when she'd
opened the door, but that wasn't true. The physical reality of Ms Jessica Gilbert now raised a hundred more
tantalising questions. But one stood out amongst all the
others?

"Did you love him?" he asked abruptly, and watched
her reactions.

Her lovely eyes rounded, her nostrils flaring in and
out as she sucked in sharply. "I don't think that's any
of your business," she bit out.

"I think it is, Ms Gilbert. My father visited his solicitor the day before he died," he went on. "His intention was to gift this place over to you. But he was killed before he could see to the transfer. He revealed that he'd been letting you live here rent-free for the past few years, but that he wanted you to have security for life."

"I see..."

Her green eyes glittered with contempt. But for whom? Luke puzzled.

"You think I was sleeping with your father for what I could get out of him," she stated coldly.

"It did cross my mind," he admitted.

"I'm sure it did. I presume *you* won't be signing this place over to me, then, will you?" she added drily.

"That depends," he said, and watched a speculative interest replace the contempt in her eyes.

"On what?" she asked carefully.

The moment she asked that question in that fashion, Luke at least knew one of the answers he'd been looking for. She *hadn't* been in love with his father. She *had* been in it for the material gain all along.

It made brutal sense. Why else would a girl as young as this be having an affair with a man as old as his father?

Luke wondered how much she'd already gleaned from him in cash during their liaison. Not to mention presents, the sort of presents rich older men gave their beautiful young mistresses. Clothes. Jewelry. Perfume. Lingerie.

She'd look incredibly sexy in black lace...

"On *what* does it depend?" she demanded to know

and, immediately, another X-rated image raised its ugly head, rattling Luke with the power this female had to both arouse and tempt him without seemingly doing a thing.

Luke stared at her and tried to imagine what she would say if he offered her this place in exchange for one weekend being *his* mistress, giving him everything she'd given his father. And more.

Oh, yes, he'd want more. He was only thirty-two years old, a man in his sexual prime, a man who hadn't made love to his fiancée in...

Guilt consumed him as his train of thought ended with Isabel: the woman he was going to marry in a fortnight's time, the woman he'd vowed always to be truthful with in future.

What was happening to him here?

Not that he'd actually *done* anything. A man could not be hung for his thoughts, especially when in the presence of the temptation sitting before him. Did she have any idea how sexy she looked, swinging her prettily painted toes in front of him, that slit in her skirt falling further and further apart till he could practically see the entire side of her left leg? And all the while she was sipping her wine and watching him over the rim of the glass like a hunter quietly watching its prey.

Luke began to understand why his father had fallen victim to her wiles. She was the devil in disguise.

At the back of his mind, Luke knew he should get the hell out of there. But his curiosity far overrode his common sense.

"It depends on your telling me all about your affair with my father," he said brusquely.

Her left leg slipped off her right knee, bringing her skirt back to a more modest arrangement. When she put her glass back down, Luke saw that her hand was shaking slightly. "*All?* What do you mean by...*all?*"

Luke liked seeing her agitated. He wasn't sure why. Perhaps because he didn't really want her to be a cold-blooded money-grubbing bitch. Luke was afraid that if she was, he might find himself in deep trouble here. For if she'd sleep with a man old enough to be her father, strictly for material gain, then what would she be capable of with *him*?

Never in Luke's life had he felt the pulling power of his dark side this much. Sure, during his years at uni, he'd sometimes acted foolishly in the sexual sense. Even recklessly. He'd been a bit of a lad over in London too, perhaps because he'd been away from his father's supposedly good influence for the first time.

But ever since he'd come back to Australia two years ago, he hadn't wanted wild sexual thrills any more. He'd wanted a more safe, secure and settled life. He'd wanted what his father had had.

Luke stared at his father's sexy young mistress and realised ruefully his dark side still wanted what his father had had. The nice little woman at home, and *this*, waiting for him at weekends.

His heart raced just thinking about it.

But they were still only just thoughts, he told himself firmly. He couldn't, he just *couldn't* act on them, no matter how tempting. He would hate himself for ever if he did.

But he still wanted to know everything about his father's affair, to try to make sense of it all.

"Exactly that," he bit out. "I want to know how and when you met my father? Who made the first move and why? How often you met and where? I want to know if he truly loved you, or just wanted you for sex. Tell me the whole rotten truth, Ms Gilbert, and this place is yours."

CHAPTER FOUR

FOR a split second Celia wanted to lash out at him. But then she saw the pain behind Luke's anger, and sympathy for him washed into her heart.

It was never nice, being confronted with a parent's fallibility, especially in matters of the flesh. Even more upsetting, at this time in his life, so soon after both his parents' tragic deaths.

"You're very angry with your father, aren't you?" she said softly.

He didn't move a muscle, except for the one twitching in his jaw.

He was more than angry. He was in a state of extreme distress. She'd sensed it the moment he'd stalked inside. His body language had been telling: the way he'd dragged out that chair, the way he'd sat down, the way he'd stared at her.

Celia picked up her glass again and drank the rest of the wine. He still didn't say a word, just kept on looking at her with those glittering black eyes. She began to feel self-conscious. No, that was a lie. She'd begun to feel self-conscious some time back, which was why she'd crossed her legs and had nervously swung her foot.

"You're very angry with me too, aren't you?" she blurted out.

"What do *you* think?" he threw back at her. "He was a married man. You didn't even love him."

Celia wished she hadn't started this, wished she'd told him the truth right from the start.

But it was too late. There was more at stake now than just protecting her mother from the pain of being grilled by Lionel's son. There was this place, which her mother deserved. She didn't have to live here. She could sell it. It would be security for her old age. Payment, for services rendered. Retribution, for want of a better word.

And if there was a measure of secret vengeance against Lionel in her decision to pretend to be his mistress, Celia didn't deny it. At the same time, she wasn't going to take the part of a callous gold-digger. Her mother hadn't been anything of the kind!

"You're wrong," Celia refuted, putting her mother's words into her own mouth. "I did love Lionel. I loved him very much."

Celia was amazed at how convincing she sounded. But then...she'd heard her mother say it often enough over the years, and had seen the way she'd looked when she said it. Celia adopted what she hoped was the same dreamy-eyed expression and waited for Luke's reaction.

Luke was amazed at how convincing she'd sounded. And how soft and warm her eyes had suddenly gone.

Was it an act? Or the truth?

"You expect me to believe that?" he said sharply.

Her green eyes cooled somewhat. "No. But you wanted the truth. That's the truth."

"If you say so. When did you first meet my father? How long ago?"

She seemed to have to think about that. "I...I was twenty-two at the time."

God, only twenty-two. And his father had been... what? Fifty!

"How old are you now?" he asked, all the while trying not to think about her at twenty-two sleeping with his fifty-year-old father.

"Twenty-six."

"Four years ago, then," he growled.

"I see your maths is excellent. But, then, you're an architect too, aren't you? Like Lionel."

"I'm my father's son," he said with an edge of irony in his voice.

"In every way," she agreed.

"What do you mean by that crack?" he snapped, and she looked genuinely taken aback. Which meant it was his own guilty mind jumping to conclusions.

"I...I only meant that you look a lot like him," she said.

Perversely, Luke began thinking that if she'd liked his father's looks, then she'd like his. And if she'd liked his father's money, then she'd like his as well. Because he had all his father's money now, as well as his own.

"How did you meet?" he asked, desperate for distraction from the darkness of his thoughts.

"At one of the wine resorts in the Hunter Valley," she answered. "Your father was there for a two-day architectural conference. I was working as a massage therapist in a few of those places at the time. Lionel booked me for a massage in his room after dinner. And the rest…as they say…is history.''

Luke struggled with the images and conclusions her curt story conjured up. He didn't want to understand his father. Nor forgive him. But what red-blooded man wouldn't have been turned on by her hands on his near naked flesh?

"Had he been drinking?'' he asked brusquely.

"He'd probably had some wine over dinner. Lionel liked his wine.''

"When did you find out he was married?''

"He confessed the next morning.''

"What did you think about that?''

"I was very upset. But I—'' She broke off, as though searching for the right words. Or was it an excuse she was looking for?

"But you *what*?'' he persisted.

"But by then I was madly in love with him,'' she finished with a sigh.

Luke snorted. "Love doesn't happen as quickly as that.''

"Maybe not to you,'' she threw at him, "but it did to me.''

This time, she wasn't nearly so convincing. Her eyes wouldn't quite meet his.

"And then what?''

Now her eyes did meet his, defiant and challenging. "I told him I could never see him again. But he wouldn't let me go.''

"What do you mean…*wouldn't*?''

"He pursued me, and he…he seduced me again.''

"Oh, for pity's sake! I don't believe he seduced you in the first place. I think *you* were the one who did the seducing."

She stared at him, startled by his accusation. "Why on earth would you think that?"

"Back at the beginning, you were only twenty-two. I know girls of twenty-two. I've dated plenty. They aren't attracted to men of fifty, even rich, relatively handsome ones. Not unless they're on the make."

She was on her feet in a shot, green eyes blazing. "Now, that's enough!" she spat out. "I won't listen to any more of your insults or answer any more of your rude questions. This place isn't worth it. So *you* keep it, and believe whatever you like. I don't give a damn. I'm out of here!"

She started marching towards the door.

He jumped to his feet, his blood all fired up as well. But for different reasons than hers. "You can't drive anywhere. You've been drinking."

She whirled, her face flushed, her eyes bright. "Then *you* get out," she demanded. "Because one of us is leaving here, or I won't be responsible for what I'll say next."

"Meaning?"

"Look," she said, clearly struggling for control, "I don't want to hurt you any more than you've been hurt by this. Believe it or not, I know what you're feeling right now."

He laughed. "You have no idea what I'm feeling right now. No idea at all! I used to hero-worship my father. I thought he was perfect. Yet here you are, telling me he was not only unfaithful to my mother, but he was a callous seducer of young girls, a sexual predator of the worst kind.''

"Close," she bit out. "You want the truth? Well, here's the truth. Your father was a bastard. A ruthless, selfish, rotten bastard. And you're right. I didn't love him. I hated him. I hated him so much I wasn't at all sorry when he died. Because it wasn't me he…he…oh…oh…oh, no!''

He watched the horror of what she'd just said register in her eyes. Her face crumpled, tears flooding into her eyes.

"I'm sorry." She sobbed. "Sorry…"

Spinning, she ran, not towards the door this time, but towards the staircase which led up to what looked like a loft bedroom. His shocked gaze followed her flight upwards till she disappeared from view, a banging door signalling that she'd sought refuge where weeping women often sought refuge.

In a bathroom.

Luke ran both his hands through his hair. They were shaking. No point in going after her. He would have to wait till she came back down.

But then…then he would *force* her to tell him the total truth!

The sound of a phone ringing startled Luke. It was not a loud ring. More of a musical one. A mobile. Not his. His was still out in his car.

Luke's eyes scanned the room and there it was, sitting on the kitchen counter. He waited impatiently for its owner to emerge from the bathroom to come down and answer it, but she didn't. She probably didn't even hear it. Luke tried to ignore the sound but he couldn't. In the end he strode over, picked the darned thing up, pressed the blue button and put it to his ear. "Yes?"

"Oh! Er…could I speak to Celia please?" A woman's voice, obviously taken aback at a man answering.

"I'm sorry," he said curtly. "There's no Celia here."

"What? Are you sure?"

"Positive. This is a Ms Gilbert's phone. Ms Jessica Gilbert. You must have rung the wrong number."

"No, I didn't," the woman refuted crisply. "I rang the right number. I have it programmed into my phone. That's Celia Gilbert's mobile you've answered, not Jessica's."

Luke frowned. Jessica must have a sister, named Celia. "Then Jessica must have borrowed Celia's mobile because the only lady in this house at the moment is a Ms *Jessica* Gilbert, not Celia."

"But that's impossible! Jessica's here with me. Right now. She's the reason I'm ringing Celia, to tell her her mother might need her to drop in some time this weekend after all. She's been asking after her."

"Her *mother*?" Luke repeated, feeling totally confused.

"Yes, her mother. I'm Helen, Jessica's older sister. And who, pray tell, are you? Some tradesman or other? Is that why you thought Celia was Jessica, because she's staying at her mother's place this weekend?"

Finally, some of the pieces of the puzzle of his father's affair slotted into place. Jessica upstairs wasn't

Jessica at all. She was Celia, Jessica's daughter. His father's mistress *hadn't* been a sexy young thing but a mature woman.

Whilst Luke preferred this picture to the one that had been troubling him severely, the fact he'd been lied to raised another very big question. *Why*, for goodness' sake?

"No," he ground out. "No, I'm not a tradesman. My name is Luke Freeman."

A horrified gasp wafted down the line, telling Luke that the woman named Helen knew exactly who he was.

"The reason I thought Celia was Jessica," he ground out, "was because she's been pretending to be Ms Jessica Gilbert ever since I arrived here a short time back."

"Oh, dear," the woman said.

"Don't hang up!" Luke ordered.

A sigh this time. "Not much point, is there? If Celia's been pretending to be Jessica then you already know my sister and your father were having an affair."

"I had my suspicions," he grated out, "which Celia more or less confirmed once she realised who I was. What I'd like to know is *why* she lied to me? Why the farce? Do you have any idea the thoughts I've had about my father, having it off with a girl young enough to be his daughter? Bad enough that he was having an affair at all!"

"Don't be angry with Celia," Helen pleaded with him. "She's very protective of her mother. Poor Jessica has had a nervous breakdown since your father died so, naturally, Celia wouldn't have wanted you coming to see her and asking her horrible questions.''

Well, yes, Luke thought grudgingly. He could understand that.

A nervous breakdown? Dad, what kind of a man *were* you? Did I ever really know you at *all*?

Luke shook his head. There was only one way to find out. He had to meet the real Ms Jessica Gilbert. ''You said this Jessica was staying with you at the moment?''

''Yes. She needs a lot of looking after. Can't do much for herself. Hardly says a word. Mostly, she just sits and stares. Or cries.''

''So where do you live, Helen? How far from Pretty Point? Can't be all that far if Celia could just drop in.''

''I'm not sure I should say. I don't want you barging in here all hot under the collar and upsetting my sister.''

''I wouldn't do that.''

''Really? You barged in there, I'll bet. Otherwise Celia would have told you the truth. There was no love lost between her and your father, I can tell you.''

''Yes. I gathered that.''

''If you don't mind my asking, what made you think your father had been having an affair in the first place? I wasn't privy to too much detail about Jessica and Lionel's relationship, but I do know he went to a lot of trouble so that his family never found out about her.''

Luke told her what had transpired at the solicitors' that day.

''I see,'' Helen murmured. ''So you're under the impression this affair has only been going on for a few years, is that it?''

"Well, yes. Of course. What…what are you trying to say?" His heart began to race in anticipation of more startling revelations.

"I hate to disillusion you further, Luke, but my sister was your father's mistress for the past twenty years."

CHAPTER FIVE

CELIA finally stopped crying and faced not only her reflection in the bathroom mirror but the fact she'd made a total mess of things downstairs.

Her blotchy cheeks and puffy eyes she could fix. Sort of. But what could she possibly tell Lionel's son to explain her outburst of hatred against his father, the man she'd supposedly loved?

Perhaps that her love had finally turned to hate because Lionel wouldn't leave his wife and marry her; that she'd realised in the end that Lionel hadn't loved her as she'd loved him. He'd just used her for sex.

Yes. Yes, maybe that would do it.

Celia would have preferred to go down there and tell the man the truth. She hated having to pretend she'd been Lionel's lover. The idea was gross. She could understand why Luke kept looking at her as he did. But on the other hand, she had to do what she could to protect her mother, and to get her this house.

Celia decided not to bother trying to fix her face other than to splash a little cold water across it. Better she went downstairs, still looking upset, with puffy eyes and dishevelled hair. After all, her lover had only died a fortnight ago. She would not be expected to be cool, calm and collected. A few hysterics were perfectly understandable.

Steeling herself, Celia opened the bathroom door, crossed the loft bedroom and slowly descended the wooden steps, glancing around with increasingly worried eyes as she did so.

Because Luke was not where she'd left him.

He was out on the deck, she soon discovered, not sitting but standing at the pine railing and staring out at the lake. His feet were apart and his hands were in his trousers pockets, the sides of his sleek suit jacket bunched up over his hips. His shoulders were slumped slightly, his body language no longer betraying anger but a type of weariness, or defeat.

A wave of sympathy washed through Celia. She'd felt sorry for him before, but not like this. Suddenly, she couldn't lie to him any more. He didn't deserve it. It wasn't right.

Nerves fluttered in her stomach as she walked over and slid back the glass door. Telling Luke she'd lied to him was going to be even harder than lying in the first place.

He spun round at the sound of the door sliding back, and stared at her again, just as intensely but not quite so angrily. Celia stared right back, for the first time seeing Luke Freeman, the man, and not just Lionel's son.

He was more handsome than his father, she realised, his face finer, his mouth softer, his dark eyes more heavily lashed. But he had his father's stubbornly squared chin, complete with dimple. And his father's hair. Thick and black and straight.

The body, too, was pure Lionel. Tall and impressive,

with broad shoulders and low slung, very slim hips. He looked a million dollars in that grey business suit, white shirt and dark red tie. But a man of his looks and build would look great in anything.

When a shiver ran down her spine, Celia frowned and crossed her arms. "It's getting chilly out there," she said from the open doorway. "Would you mind coming back inside? I have something I have to say to you."

He shrugged and withdrew his hands from his trouser pockets, the elegant grey jacket flapping shut again. "If you insist," he said, and began walking towards her. She stepped back just in time, but his right arm still brushed against hers as he entered the room, sending an electric current right down to her fingertips.

Celia smothered the gasp that rose to her lips, standing there frozen for a few seconds while she watched him walk over and settle himself on the sofa in front of the fireplace.

Not cold, she realised. Chemistry. Sexual chemistry.

Celia shouldn't have been shocked. Luke Freeman was a very handsome man, the sort who would have female hearts a-thumping whenever he walked into a room. But good grief, the last man on earth she wanted to be attracted to was Lionel's son! Mother nature had a very peculiar and extremely perverse sense of humour.

With a blackly frustrated sigh, she shut the door and walked over to stand on the rug, facing him, her back to the fireplace.

Be businesslike, she told herself. And firm. Don't waffle. Or make excuses. Just tell him the truth.

*   *   *

Luke looked up at her and wondered what lies she was going to feed him now.

He wasn't angry with her any more. He understood full well why she'd done what she'd done. But he was curious as to how far she would go to protect her mother.

"I have to apologise," she began, surprising him.

"For what, exactly?"

"I lied to you," she stated, impressing him now. It took courage to admit to lying.

"What about?"

"I'm not your father's mistress," she stated boldly and rather bravely, he thought. "And my name's not Jessica. It's Celia. If you recall, when you first arrived you asked me if I was a Ms Gilbert and I said yes, because I am. But I'm *Celia* Gilbert. Jessica Gilbert is my mother."

Any idea he had to string her along went out the window.

"I know," he said.

She blinked her shock. "Huh?"

Time for *him* to be honest. "While you were upstairs in the bathroom, your Aunt Helen rang. I answered your phone. She asked for Celia. I told her there was no Celia here, only a Jessica. She told me that was impossible because Jessica was there, with her. I think you can fill in the rest, don't you?"

"Oh..." Stunned, she stumbled over and sank down on the other end of the sofa. "How...how much did she tell you?"

"Enough," he said. "Yet not enough."

She gnawed at her bottom lip, bringing his attention to how full it was, how full *both* her lips were. Her not being his father's mistress hadn't stopped the X-rated thoughts at all.

He'd thought… He'd hoped…

Luke shook his head. He'd been wrong, blast it.

"What *did* Aunt Helen tell you?" she asked, her lovely eyes worried.

Luke recalled her aunt's bitter relaying of the facts over the phone.

"Jessica was twenty-two when she met your father. She was a single mum with a six-year-old-girl at the time, struggling to make ends meet by giving massages at resorts in the Hunter Valley to wealthy businessmen and tourists. She was living in a pokey two-room flat in Maitland and drove a car which should have been condemned. Despite all that, she was the most beautiful girl, both inside and out.

"But that's still no excuse for your father. He knew he was married with a son when he first met Jessica. But she didn't know that till after she'd spent the night with him and, by then, she was deeply in love. She tried to give him up but simply couldn't. He wouldn't let her. He kept coming back and coming back, bringing little Celia gifts and telling Jessica how much he loved her, as well as other lies. In the end, Jessica was so besotted with him that she did whatever he wanted. And what he wanted was her at his beck and call, but with total secrecy and discretion. They managed that at Jessica's place till Celia grew up enough to know what was going on. I gather the poor child made quite a scene one day.

But did they have the decency to stop then? Good heavens, no. After that, Jessica was always running all over the countryside, meeting up with your father in remote motels for a few wretched hours. Then there was this grotty little fishing cabin they spent weekends in sometimes. I don't know where. Lionel finally built the place you're in at this moment and set her up there. A love nest, Jessica called it. A lust nest more like it!''

There'd been more of the same. Clearly, Lionel hadn't been a favourite with Aunt Helen. Her sister's behaviour hadn't been too popular, either.

Luke decided a briefer, less venomous version was called for.

''I know how long the affair's been going on,'' he admitted. ''I know your mother's circumstances when they met. I know she loved my father a lot.''

''Did Aunt Helen say that?'' She looked amazed.

''No,'' he confessed drily. ''When I questioned her about that, she used words such as sexual obsession and infatuation. But why else would your mother have a breakdown, if her caring hadn't been very real, and very deep?''

Celia threw him a grateful look. ''It was,'' she said, sighing. ''Too deep.''

''Is that why you pretended to be your mother? Because of her fragile emotional state?''

''Yes.''

''You didn't want me talking to her.''

''That's right.''

''But you still wanted me to leave her this house.''

She grimaced, then shot him a pleading glance. ''I

thought she deserved...something. When he was alive, she never took anything from your father. Not anything of any value, anyway,'' she added. ''She always supported herself. Lionel bought her some little gifts over the years and, more recently, he let her live here rent-free. He might have slipped her a few dollars every now and then, but only for food or wine or whatever other creature comforts he himself enjoyed during the time he spent here. But that's not much in exchange for almost a lifetime of loving and sacrifice. Not that Mum ever asked for anything from Lionel. The only thing she ever wanted from your father was his love.''

''I gather you and your Aunt Helen don't think she ever really got that.''

Her spine stiffened. ''That's right,'' she said tartly. ''We don't.''

''What about your mother herself? What did she think?''

''She thought he loved her. Apparently, he used to say he did. But men often say that to get sex, don't they?'' she added bitterly.

''Do they?'' He looked deep into her eyes and wondered if that had been *her* experience, men telling her they loved her to have sex with her. If they did, he could well understand it.

She glanced away from his probing gaze and stood up. ''I think I could do with some coffee. Would you like some? Or tea? There's still some white wine left in the bottle, if you'd prefer. It's Chablis.''

If he started drinking, things could go from bad to

worse. He might do something really dreadful, rather than just think about it.

"Coffee would be great, thanks. White. No sugar."

She hurried over to the kitchen, relieved, he thought, to put some distance between them. Maybe she was aware of the rampant desire that smouldered within him every time he looked at her. And it frightened her. It frightened him. He'd never felt anything like it.

He watched her silently make the coffee, never glancing over his way. Deliberately, he wondered? Or was she just lost in thought?

He wished he could stop himself looking at her but he couldn't. He swivelled round in the corner of the sofa to keep her in view, his eyes following her every movement.

"Are you a dancer?" he asked at last.

Her head jerked up, her green eyes startled. "No. Why? What made you think that?"

"The way you look. The way you move."

She laughed, as women do when they're both embarrassed and pleased at the same time. "Sorry. No, I'm not a dancer, though I do like dancing. I'm a physiotherapist. It's what my mother always wanted to be but she never had the proper training. She's a darned good masseuse, though."

"And you? Are you a darned good masseuse?"

She shrugged. "I'm an efficient one."

He wallowed for a few moments in the idea of her hands on his naked flesh.

Big mistake! He shifted uncomfortably on the sofa. "Er...where do you practise your physiotherapy?"

"I'm managing a sports injury clinic over at Swansea at the moment. The owner's away on maternity leave."

"You like your job?"

"Most days. Though it's not quite as rewarding as my previous one. I used to work with accident victims in various hospitals around the Central Coast, but it got me down in the end, especially when children were involved and things didn't go right. Still, I might go back to that kind of work when I'm older. And tougher."

"You could never be tough," he said and she smiled a wry little smile.

"I'm tougher than I look. Trust me. Would you like something with your coffee?"

You, he thought.

His teeth clenched hard in his jaw. Stop it, Luke, he ordered himself.

But how *did* one stop your mind from thinking things?

"There's not much here at the moment," she added, whilst he did his best to look innocent, and not like the closet lech he'd suddenly become. "No cake, just some biscuits. I didn't realise the cupboards were so bare."

"I don't want anything else for now. Just the coffee."

She brought his mug of coffee over and set it on the side table next to his left arm. Unfortunately, this required her leaning over. Far too close to him for comfort.

The sight of her braless breasts swinging away from her chest wall and forming a temporary but most tantalising cleavage barely inches from his face did things to Luke's body that could only be described as sadistic. He immediately sat up straighter, and when she turned to walk away he swept up the mug and cradled it in his hands over his lap.

She sat back down at the other end of the sofa and sipped her coffee, not looking his way, thank goodness. She was, instead, staring blankly ahead into the dead hearth of the fireplace.

"By the way," he said, "your Aunt Helen said to tell you your mother's been asking for you, so you might have to drop in on her this weekend after all."

She nodded slowly, sadly.

"How bad is she?" he asked, happy to be feeling sympathy for her rather than desire.

She shook her head. "Not good. She hardly speaks. She's very depressed. She has nightmares. Sometimes, in her sleep, she'll cry and call out Lionel's name."

"Ah…" Luke still found it hard to see his father as the kind of man who could ruthlessly and selfishly destroy another woman's life. But that was what he'd done, whether he'd meant to or not. Luke could understand his father being overcome by a moment's passion when he'd been away from home—especially if Celia's mother was half as beautiful as Celia—but he should have walked away after that first night. He should never have come back. The emotional damage he'd done to that innocent mother and child over the years must have been horrendous.

He thought of what Celia's Aunt Helen had told him about his father's coming back time after time, showering gifts on Celia as a child, playing at being her father for a day then disappearing again, possibly for weeks on end. No wonder Celia hated him with a passion. She'd probably loved him once, as lonely needy children loved grown-ups who were kind to them.

But once she'd started to grow up herself and had seen the situation for what it was, she'd recognised the hypocrisy of the man, and her love had turned to hate.

"I'm so sorry, Celia," he said softly. "So very, very sorry. My father has a lot to answer for. I have no excuses for him. What he did was very wrong. But your mother's not the only person he hurt over the past twenty years, is she?"

Their eyes met across the length of the sofa. "What…what do you mean? Your mother didn't know. *Did* she?"

Luke was taken aback by Celia's question, raising sudden doubts of his own.

Till now he'd clung to the fact that his mother had not known about her husband's affair, and would now never know. It would have broken her heart if she'd discovered her beloved Lionel had been unfaithful to her.

But what if she *had* known? Perhaps that was why he'd caught her looking so sad sometimes for no apparent reason, why she'd suffered those dreadful migraines.

No, no, that didn't make sense. His father hadn't met Jessica till Luke had been twelve and his mother had had migraines for as far back as he could remember. As for her looking sad sometimes, everyone suffered some small bouts of depression. It wasn't possible to be happy all the time.

He was imagining things.

"For what it's worth," Celia said swiftly, "Mum's very sure your mother didn't know about them. I didn't mean to imply differently. It was just that you said my mother was not the only one Lionel hurt and I thought…I mean…" She shrugged, clearly a bit confused.

Luke nodded. "It's all right. I'm sure she didn't know too. I was talking about you, Celia. My father hurt you as well."

Celia stared at him, her green eyes wide with surprise.

"Dad's not here to apologise for his reprehensible behaviour," Luke went on, "so I'd like to do so on his behalf. I'm sure he didn't mean to hurt you, Celia. He loved children. But he did hurt you, all the same, and I feel really rotten about it."

"Oh…" She looked stricken by his sympathetic words. Her chin began to wobble and so did her hands, a couple of spots of hot coffee spilling into her lap.

"Oh!" she cried, then burst into tears.

Luke didn't stop to think. He acted, hurriedly putting down his mug of coffee and sliding down the sofa to pry hers out of her suddenly shaking hands before more coffee was spilt. He had to lean over her to put her mug down on the other side table, but there was no sexual intent in the physical contact. Luke was just being what he basically was: a gentleman.

When he straightened, however, he was sitting right

beside her, their sides jammed up against each other. Before he could safely retreat, she swivelled and buried her face into his chest, clutching the lapels of his jacket and sobbing piteously.

Panic—and possibly something else—set Luke's heart pounding. What was a man to do?

Run, came the common-sense command.

But how could he? She needed comforting. And there was no one else.

Luke squeezed his eyes shut, prayed for salvation, and put his arms around her.

CHAPTER SIX

CELIA soon stopped clutching his lapels and sank into the warmth of his solid embrace, the side of her head pressed against the wall of his chest, her arms sliding underneath his suit jacket and around his back where she hugged him tightly, never wanting to let him go.

How good it felt to be held like this, she thought even as she wept. How good for someone to finally understand how angry and frustrated she'd been over the years, watching her mother throwing her life away on a married man.

Her mother had never understood, especially not once Celia had left home. She'd told her to go and make her own life and to stop worrying about hers.

That Lionel Freeman's son would understand was amazing.

How nice he was. How kind. How...*strong*, she suddenly realised when his arms tightened around her.

He must work out, she began thinking as her fingertips moved across his back, feeling the bunched muscles beneath them, admiring their shape and their power.

He moaned, a startlingly tormented sound which brought her head up, her eyes searching his in bewilderment.

They glittered back down at her.

"You shouldn't have touched me like that," he

growled, one hand coming up to cup her chin. "I'm only human, Celia. Only human…" And he held her face captive while his mouth crashed down on hers.

Celia's first instinct was to struggle. Because this was Lionel's son kissing her. *Lionel's* son!

But then his tongue slipped past her startled lips and Celia's heart stopped beating.

Dear heaven, she thought dazedly.

When her heart finally kicked back to life there was no further thought of struggling. There was nothing but surrender.

She melted against him, wallowing in the warm, wet pleasure of his tongue dancing with hers. When his mouth lifted momentarily, she groaned in protest. He muttered something unintelligible then tipped her head back over his arm and clamped his lips to the soft skin at the base of her throat, sucking on it like some ravenous beast.

Celia finally understood why some women found vampire films erotic. Her moans carried no pain. Just pleasure. Primitive primal pleasure.

When his free hand found a breast, her senses reeled further, her nipple peaking hard against the heat of his palm. When his hand splayed wide and he rubbed the surface of his taut skin over the rock-like peak, the sensations were exquisite.

Too soon, his hand fell away, and she groaned in dismay. Not so when it slid inside her skirt and sought to stroke her between her thighs. Now she gasped, her knees instinctively parting to give him better access to the molten fire that already awaited him there. At first he caressed her over her panties, but finally his fingers slipped underneath the elastic.

Celia had never felt anything like it. She cried out, her back arching as her body raced towards a climax. Never, with any other man, had this happened to her so quickly.

His hand suddenly stilled, his head lifting from her throat. Their eyes met and, whilst his looked pained, Celia knew hers had to be reflecting sheer desperation.

"Don't stop," she pleaded breathlessly.

He laughed an odd sort of laugh, scooping her up with him as he stood up. "Your wish is my command, beautiful. But not here. If I'm going to do this, and it seems I am," he added ruefully as he carried her towards the stairs, "then I might as well be hung for a sheep as a lamb."

He mounted the wooden steps two at a time, bringing them swiftly to the loft bedroom where her mother and his father must have made love hundreds of times.

It was spacious but sparsely furnished, with a huge bed in the middle of the polished floor, and colourfully woven rugs on three sides. The foot of the bed faced a wall of sliding glass doors that led out onto another deck overlooking the lake. There was a walk-in wardrobe built into one sloping side wall and a bathroom set into the other.

Celia had stripped the bed and had put her own sheets and duvet on when she'd arrived that afternoon, not feeling comfortable with the remnants of Lionel's distinctive cologne pervading the bedclothes.

If anyone had told her then, that in a couple of hours

she would be about to make love with Lionel Freeman's son on that same bed, she would have called them insane. Yet here she was, in Luke's arms, breathless with anticipation, excited beyond all words, feverish in her desire to be naked on that bed with him.

Talk about ironic!

At least she now had more understanding of why her mother had acted as she had. If Lionel had made her feel anything like this, it would have been very difficult to send him away, married or not?

This last thought brought a jab of panic.

"You're not married, are you?" she asked him anxiously as he approached the bed.

He ground to a halt and stared down at her for a few excruciatingly long moments. "No," he said at last. "Are you?"

"Of course not!"

He smiled, a darkly enigmatic smile. "Of course not," he repeated, and laid her down across the bed.

He straightened to stare down at her for several seconds, then bent to slide his hands up her legs under her skirt and pull down her black cotton panties.

Celia's eyes had grown very round by the time they slipped off her feet.

He tossed her panties aside then began to take off his own clothes, starting with his jacket and tie. She just lay there, watching him with wide eyes, her heart beating like jungle drums, her face flushed with excitement. He walked over to the one and only chair in the room, draping his jacket and tie over the back before sitting down to remove his shoes and socks.

This done, he stood up again and walked back over to stand by the bed, looking down at her.

"Undo the buttons on your top," he said as he began undoing *his* shirt buttons.

There was no thought of refusing him, though her hands did fumble a bit as she worked her way down the six black buttons. When she'd undone the last one, she hesitated. He'd undone his last button as well but hadn't removed his shirt. His hands had dropped back to his sides and his focus was all on her.

"Open it," he commanded.

She took a breath and opened the cardigan, baring her braless breasts to his avid eyes.

He stared, and her already erect nipples tightened further.

"Now your skirt," he ordered. "Don't take it off. Open it. Wide."

Celia sucked in sharply. She'd never known anything so wickedly thrilling. Yet he was only looking at her.

She parted her skirt and pulled the sides back, exposing all her legs plus the triangle of dark curls between them.

"And now...your legs," he said, his voice as thick as syrup.

Celia's head spun. Her legs... He wanted her to open her legs... Wanted to see where she was wet with desire for him...

She couldn't. Surely not. She'd die of embarrassment.

She opened her legs, and didn't die of embarrassment. She felt shockingly alive and incredibly turned on.

His eyes glittered wildly and heat washed all through her. As did a fierce longing. Looking at her there wasn't nearly enough. She wanted his hands there. His mouth. His tongue. Just the thought of such things made her light-headed. Her thighs quivered and her heartbeat quickened.

"Luke, please," she choked out.

"I won't be long," he promised and reefed open his shirt, tossing it aside.

Celia stared at the beauty of him and was besieged by even more needs. Not just to be touched but to do the touching herself. She was dying to run her hands over his magnificent chest and shoulders, to tangle her fingers in the thatch of dark curls that covered the centre of his chest, following them down to where they disappeared beyond his waistband, that waistband that Luke was at that very moment snapping undone.

She watched, mouth drying, as he unzipped his fly and dragged his trousers off, revealing snug black briefs that were straining to encompass the evidence of *his* desire. Celia tried to imagine how it would feel when he entered her and her insides clenched down hard at the thought. He was big, she could see. Bigger than any other man she'd been with.

Would that make a difference? she wondered breathlessly. Did size *really* matter?

Celia was wallowing in the thought that she would soon know when Luke bent to pull his wallet from his discarded trousers and, from there, a condom.

"I've only got the one with me," he muttered, dropping the wallet on the floor. "That'll have to do."

Celia stared at him for a moment, doing her best to find excuses for herself for not even thinking about protection before this. Normally, she was so insistent about practising safe sex. Making sure a condom was going to be used was usually her number one priority before going to bed with any of her previous boyfriends.

But the truth was she'd have let Luke have her down there on the sofa, without protection. She'd have probably let him have her up here as well. Okay, so perhaps, at the back of her mind, she already knew that the odds of her conceiving today were less than zero. Her period was due early next week.

But still…pregnancy was not the only problem associated with having sex these days.

Thank goodness Luke wasn't quite as carried away as she was.

Or was he? His hands were shaking as he tossed his wallet aside, then he dropped his underpants.

Celia blinked, then swallowed. He *was* big. She hoped the condom would fit.

In the past, she'd never actually watched any man putting on protection. But she watched Luke, her awed eyes feasting on his flesh, anticipating the pleasure of his possession. If this man didn't satisfy her, then no man ever could.

Because no man had. Not once. Not properly.

But when he finally stepped up to the bed between her spread knees, Celia had one last depressing thought. Maybe Luke's size or abilities as a lover weren't going to make a blind bit of difference. Maybe her coming or not coming during sex *was* all her fault. Maybe she just wasn't capable of coming that way. End of story.

His hands scooped under her bare buttocks and pulled her abruptly towards him. No more foreplay, she realised with a degree of shock as he angled himself into her. Just him, driving home to the hilt, then pumping powerfully, each stroke of his swollen flesh twisting her insides tighter and tighter like a coiled spring. This is it, she thought elatedly. But when several minutes passed with no orgasm happening, her ecstasy turned to agony.

She moaned, her head thrashing from side to side, her eyes squeezing tightly shut, her face grimacing in eternal frustration. She was never going to come. Never!

His pulling out brought a startled cry of dismay.

"Trust me," he told her and flipped her over, pushing her skirt up out of the way and hoisting her up onto her knees. Her face flamed momentarily with a fierce embarrassment. How must she look to him like that? But he was inside her again in no time, and any qualms were soon obliterated by the heat of the moment.

It felt fantastic his doing it to her like that. Wickedly wantonly fantastic!

She began to moan quite loudly, muffling the mortifying sounds by pressing her face into the mattress. Her hands clutched the duvet on either side of her head and everything spun way, way out of control. No thoughts of failure now. No thoughts at all. Just heat and sex. Raw animal sounds. His. Hers.

Their bodies exploded together, his hips shuddering

to a halt whilst hers rocked wildly back and forth against him.

"More," she muttered through clenched teeth when the spasms of blinding pleasure began to fade. "More."

But soon, there was no more. There was nothing but an emotion-charged stillness. She could still hear his ragged breathing. And her own. But he wasn't moving a muscle, and neither was she.

His withdrawal from her body was so abrupt she cried out.

"No more," he ground out. "*Definitely* no more. This was a mistake. A big mistake."

Celia remained frozen where she was.

"Hell," he muttered, forcefully pressing her flat on the bed and yanking her skirt down over her naked bottom. "I'm sorry, Celia. Sorry..."

By the time a stunned Celia rolled over, he was already disappearing into the bathroom and banging the door shut behind him.

For a few moments, she just lay there, staring at the bathroom door. It was almost impossible to think straight when her body was still thrumming with the aftermath of their torrid lovemaking and that nerve-numbing climax. But eventually, the reality of what she'd just done with Luke sank in.

Celia rolled back over and buried her face into the bed. What must he think of her?

And what did she think of herself, going to bed with him so soon after meeting him?

It wasn't like her to do that. It wasn't like her to feel

what she'd felt with him, either. Or to make love in such a flagrantly provocative position.

But, oh, it had been wonderful with Luke, hadn't it? As for that orgasm…talk about mind-blowing! Despite feeling shock at her boldness, Celia couldn't help being thrilled that her never coming before hadn't been her fault after all. It seemed all she'd needed was the right man, with the right moves.

Still, the fact that Lionel Freeman's son should be that right man was shocking in itself. Fate really did have a perverse sense of humour.

The sound of the toilet flushing sent Celia rolling back over to stare at the bathroom door. Her heart started to pound as she waited for Luke to emerge again. But he didn't. Instead, she heard the shower being snapped on.

Celia had to confess to being relieved. She needed a few more minutes to think before facing Luke again. Above all, she wanted to work out just why he thought making love to her was such a big mistake?

Was it because of the speed and impulsiveness of their encounter? Or simply because of who she was? His father's mistress's daughter.

Perhaps. He might also think, for the very same reason, that their exploring a further relationship was out of the question.

But how could he turn his back on the incredible sex they'd just shared? The passion! The pleasure!

Celia knew she couldn't. She wanted Luke to come back to this bed and make more wonderful love to her. Yet it seemed he wasn't going to do that. Strange, when most men would have jumped at the chance. What was the real problem here? It had to be more than just who they were. There had to be something else...

"Oh!" Celia gasped, her heart lurching. "Oh, no."

How stupid of her not to realise! A man like Luke. Handsome. Rich. Clever. Eligible. There was no way there wouldn't be some woman in his life. Maybe not a wife. But certainly a girlfriend of some kind.

That was why he'd called their making love a big mistake. Because he was already involved with someone else!

She stared at the door that separated them and tried to be angry with him. But she wasn't. How strange. She should have been angry. She should have been furious!

Yet all she felt was despair...

The sounds of the shower gushing on and on gradually began to get under her skin, as did his washing himself totally clean of her before returning to Sydney.

The thought of his going back to another woman's bed tonight finally brought anger. Plus the bleakest, blackest jealousy.

She couldn't let him get away with that, not without being made to face her and tell her the truth!

Celia scrambled off the bed and headed for the bathroom door, hurriedly fixing her clothes as she went.

CHAPTER SEVEN

LUKE leant with his hands and head against the shower wall and groaned. He was no better than his father, really, was he? Making love to a girl without telling her the truth about himself.

When she'd asked him if he was married, he shouldn't have said no. He should have said shortly.

But of course saying shortly would have dashed it for him, wouldn't it? And he hadn't wanted that. Not right at that precise moment. He'd wanted her, how he'd wanted her.

He still wanted her, he conceded, glancing downwards. Once hadn't been nearly enough.

Gritting his teeth, he reached to snap off the hot tap. But, even as the water turned cold and the icy spray painfully pummelled his body, he kept thinking about her. The way she'd done everything he'd asked. The way she'd trusted him when he'd turned her over.

She shouldn't have. He wasn't worthy of her trust.

The shower door sliding back frightened the life out of him. He jerked around and there she stood, his nemesis, her beautiful green eyes blazing, her arms crossed over her chest, her lovely hair falling down around her very angry face.

The buttons on her top, he noted, had been refastened, but into the wrong slots. And her skirt was still askew. There was a purplish love bite at the base of her neck, only partially covered by her hair.

"You have a girlfriend back in Sydney, don't you?" she threw at him. "That's why you're sorry. That's why you said making love to me was a big mistake."

Luke turned off the shower and did his best to look dignified. Difficult when he was naked and freezing, and not nearly limp enough.

"Hand me a towel, will you?" he asked in what he hoped was a coolly commanding tone.

She glowered at him. "Here." She snatched one of the white towels off the towel rail and shoved it into his stomach.

He grunted, then wrapped the towel very firmly around his hips because the last thing he wanted was the darned thing to fall off. "Shall we go back out into the bedroom?" he suggested with seeming calm.

"Oh, by all means," she snapped. "Let's return to the scene of the crime."

"I haven't committed a crime, Celia. A mistake, yes. But not a crime."

"That's just semantics, and you know it." She whirled and marched back out into the bedroom, with him following. Once he got there, however, Luke wished he'd stayed in the bathroom. Just looking at that bed reminded him of how she'd looked, lying spread-eagled for him, so turned on she simply *couldn't* have said no to him.

Suddenly, he felt afraid, afraid of what he might say to turn her on like that again so that he could make her do all those other things a man wants a woman to do when he desires her this much.

But if he ever set about seducing her again, ruthlessly and without regard to her feelings, he really would be no better than his father.

He had to tell her the truth. And quickly. For his own sake as well as hers.

"Yes," he admitted. "I have a girlfriend."

She made a tiny whimpering sound of distress that stung his conscience.

"I'm sorry, Celia," he said sincerely. "All I can say in my defence is that I didn't mean any of this to happen. I was only trying to comfort you when I took you in my arms. As I said before, you're a very beautiful girl, and I'm only human."

She sank down on the side of the bed as though dazed, her hurt eyes still on him. "What's her name?"

"Isabel."

"Isabel," she repeated, and just kept staring at him. "Do...do you live with her?"

"No."

"Do you have a date with her tonight?"

"No."

He saw the flicker of relief in her eyes and realised with a degree of self-disgust that she'd been worried he would go straight from her bed to Isabel's. Obviously, after the way his father had treated her mother, Celia expected men to behave badly. Guilt consumed Luke when he recalled the comment she'd made about how men often lied to get sex. He hadn't lied directly, but he had by omission.

"Are you serious about each other?" she asked, and he stiffened. He didn't want to hurt her any more than necessary. Surely it would serve no purpose for her to know he was engaged.

"We've been dating for quite a while," he hedged. "I met her at work late last year."

"I see…" She fell silent then, her shoulders sagging, her head drooping. Luke had never felt so rotten in his entire life. He dared not go to her and touch her in any way, but he felt compelled to let her know how special he thought she was.

"What we shared, Celia," he said gently, "it was…amazing. I'll always remember you. Always."

Her head lifted, and a sad little smile played on her lips. "And I you, Luke Freeman. Do you know that was the first time I've ever come during sex?"

He stared at her. Did she have to tell him that?

"You don't believe me?"

"I…I'm surprised, that's all."

She stood up abruptly. "You'd better get dressed. I'll go downstairs and leave you to it."

Celia somehow made it downstairs before dissolving into tears. She cried quietly, afraid that if she surrendered to sobbing, he would hear it up in the loft. Finally, she fled out onto the deck, tears streaming down her face, her thoughts as tormenting as her emotions.

He had a girlfriend. Named Isabel. Probably an architect, like him. Some superintelligent, stunningly sophisticated creature who would never admit to him that she'd never climaxed during sex before.

Celia knew, without being told, that she simply could

not compete—or compare—with this Isabel. Even her name was superior. Celia was such an old-fashioned name. Isabel sounded coolly stylish and elegant, like its owner, no doubt.

Celia looked down at herself and groaned. How could Luke possibly call her beautiful? She was a mess. Her hair. Her clothes. Her face.

Flattery, she supposed. Men were such good liars.

She dashed the tears from her cheeks with the back of her hands then pulled the remaining pins from her hair, letting it tumble around her shoulders. She fixed the buttons on her top then yanked her skirt around straight. Not a good move, the action reminding her she was still naked underneath.

Her face flamed when she thought of how obedient she'd been. How...willing.

"Now your skirt... Open it," he'd said. "Wide.

"And now...your legs..."

Her mouth dried at the memory and her legs shifted slightly apart. She gripped the railing and thought of how it would feel if he were inside her now.

"Celia?"

She spun round at the sound of his voice, her face flushing guiltily as though she'd been caught doing something indecent.

Luke tried not to ogle her. But she was a tempting sight with that glorious hair of hers down on her shoulders. He ached to reach out and touch it, to wind it through his fingers and pull her head back, baring her neck to him again. He couldn't see the mark on her throat any more but he knew it was there.

His mark. *His* brand. *His* woman.

The fierce possessiveness of his thoughts shook him.

He really wished she hadn't told him he'd been the first man to satisfy her. That kind of thing was bound to stroke a man's ego, and tempt his dark side.

Such knowledge would make it so very easy to seduce her again. He only had to step forward and take her into his arms, tell her he'd break up with Isabel, then start kissing her. She wouldn't stand a chance.

Luke cleared his throat. Definitely time to go.

"I'll have the solicitor mail the deed of this property to your mother as soon as possible," he said. "If you could just give me her current address?"

"I'll write it down for you."

Celia walked towards where he was standing in the doorway and waited for him to turn and go back inside. But he didn't, and for one ghastly moment she thought he was going to reach out and pull her into his arms once more. It wasn't that he made a move, but there was something in his eyes. A sudden predatory gleam.

She sucked in sharply and glared at him.

"Don't you dare touch me!"

"I wasn't going to," he denied.

"Then, step back," she ordered, and he did.

Celia hurried past him and headed straight for the drawer in the kitchen where she knew there was a pen and a note pad. She was leaning on the counter and writing down Aunt Helen's address when her mobile phone began to ring. It was barely inches from her hands but she kept on writing and the phone kept on ringing.

"Shouldn't you answer it?" Luke said, an edge in his voice. "It might be *your* boyfriend."

Celia blinked up at him. "*My* boyfriend?"

"It came to me just now that there has to be one. A girl like you wouldn't be wanting for admirers. Or dates."

"There is no current boyfriend," she returned brusquely. "I gave up on them some time back. In fact, I gave up on the whole male species. Pity I made an exception for you today. The trouble was I thought you were different. But you aren't different at all. You just have better moves than most. Now, if you'll excuse me?"

Celia banged down the pen and snatched up the mobile. "Yes?"

"Celia, it's Aunt Helen."

"Oh, yes, Aunt Helen. I got your message. I was going to come over later night, after you've had dinner. I didn't want to put you to any trouble. Is that all right?"

"Is Lionel's son still there?"

"What? Well…er…yes. But he was just leaving," she added, glowering over at him.

"Could I talk to him first please?"

"What about?" Celia was instantly wary.

"I have this idea."

"What idea?"

"It's about your mother. Look, I didn't want to worry you but her depression is much worse today. She's finally come to the conclusion that Lionel didn't love her at all. Pity she didn't realise that twenty years ago but there's nothing we can do about that now.''

True, Celia thought bitterly.

''I was wondering if it wouldn't do her some good to see and talk to Lionel's son. I know he wanted to talk to her and, having talked to him myself, I'm sure he won't say anything nasty. I think he's just curious to meet her, and you can understand that. Anyway, perhaps he could tell her about his father wanting to leave her their little love nest at the same time. Maybe that will reassure her that his dad did care for her in more than a sexual sense. She needs *some* kind of reassurance, believe me. And neither of us can give it to her.''

Celia knew what her aunt was saying made sense, but the thought of spending more time with Luke made her very tense. ''Luke didn't mention to you that he's intending to gift this place over to Mum himself?'' she said.

''No! Oh, how marvellous! That's even better. Jessica really loves that place, you know. In that case, why don't the two of you come over for dinner? John's working the early nightshift at the plant and won't be here. It'll just be the four of us, though I'm not sure your mother will come down from her room. She's taken to having a meal on a tray all by herself. What time is it now? Sixish. I'll make dinner for seven-thirty. Come any time after seven.''

''I'll have to ask Luke first, Aunt Helen.''

''Oh, yes. Yes, of course.''

Celia covered the phone with her hand and turned to him.

"Ask me what?" he said with a worried frown on his far too handsome face.

Celia told him her aunt's suggestion.

"So what do you think?" she asked when he stayed silent and frowning.

"I'll do it on one condition."

"What's that?"

"We take our own cars, so I can drive back to Sydney straight afterwards."

She stared at his grim expression and realised he was afraid to be alone with her. *Afraid.*

It was a telling revelation. And a terribly tempting one. Luke had already confessed that he found her beautiful, and that he was only human.

Well…she was only human too…

"Unfortunately, that's not possible," she said. "You'll have to drive me. When you were getting dressed just now I had another glass of wine. My nerves were rather shot at the time."

It was a lie. Her first of many, she imagined. Now *she* was afraid, afraid of what she was prepared to do to get this man into bed with her again. No wonder there was a saying that all was fair in love and war, she thought. Because when you were in love, you…

Celia managed not to gasp in shock, nor to look too taken aback. But she was rattled all the same. This *couldn't* be love she felt for Luke. It was just sex. No one fell in love as quickly as that. Except perhaps romantic fools like her mother.

But if that was the case, why did the idea of his

leaving her and going back to Isabel bother her so much?

It didn't just bother her. It made her go crazy inside. This had to be love. Had to be!

You *are* just like your mother, came the shattering realisation. When the right man came along, you fell hard and fast and you'll do anything to keep him. Anything at all!

As Celia looked at Luke with her newly opened eyes, her initial shock swiftly changing to a stubborn resolve. She might be like her mother in some ways, but she wasn't going to end up like her mother. No way!

But she would have to be bold to get what she wanted. Luke wasn't married yet. He wasn't even engaged. And he didn't love this Isabel. If he did, he would have said so. He also wouldn't have fallen into bed with her so fast, if he'd been really in love with someone else.

As much as Celia was a bit cynical about men and sex, she felt sure Luke wasn't that type of man. His horror at his father's behaviour had been genuine. No, Luke was basically a straight shooter, not a deceiver.

She figured he had to be fiercely attracted to her to have done what he'd done this afternoon. If he fancied her that much in old clothes and with no make-up on, then wait till he saw her tonight!

She'd brought one decent outfit with her. She *always* took one decent outfit with her whenever she went away anywhere for a couple of days. On top of that, there was so much more she could do with her face and hair.

Add some jewelry and a dash of perfume, and she would knock him for six!

"All right?" she said, cool on the outside but feverishly determined on the inside. She wasn't going to spend the rest of her life with a broken heart. She was going to win this man. He *was* different, she believed. Different from his father. Different from every man she'd ever known.

"I suppose so," he replied reluctantly. "It's not far, is it?"

"Only ten minutes or so. He said that's fine," she told her Aunt Helen crisply. "Expect us there between seven and seven-thirty. I have to shower and change first. I'm a bit of a mess."

Luke looked more worried than ever.

"Should I tell Jessica in advance who you're bringing?" Aunt Helen asked.

"No," Celia returned swiftly. "She'll panic. The reason I was able to get her out of this place so quickly was because she was afraid Luke might turn up and jump to all the right conclusions. Lionel did a good job of brainwashing her that secrecy was their number one priority."

She saw Luke wince and knew he felt guilty over keeping Isabel a secret today. Good, she thought. It showed he had a conscience. Nothing like his father.

"Don't tell her I'm bringing anyone at all," Celia warned her aunt. "I'll go up to her room when I first get there and explain. I don't want her answering the door or seeing Luke till I do that, all right?"

"If you say so, but it seems a bit cloak-and-daggerish."

"Maybe so, but it's a necessary precaution because when Mum meets Luke she's in for a real shock."

"In what way?"

"He's the dead spit of Lionel, twenty years ago."

CHAPTER EIGHT

"WHICH way now?" Luke asked brusquely as they approached a roundabout.

"Turn right," Celia directed. "Then just follow that road. It'll take you through Morisset and over the railway line then straight to Dora Creek. It's not far. Just a few kilometres."

Luke followed her directions in a grim silence, not at all happy with the situation. As much as he *did* want to see and talk to the woman who'd obviously held his father in thrall for an amazing twenty years, his need to flee the presence of her equally seductive daughter had become far greater during the last fifteen minutes.

Celia had disappeared up into the loft after the phone call from her Aunt Helen, claiming she was only going to freshen up. But she had swanned down a full hour later, looking—and smelling—far too enticing for words.

Green was undoubtedly her colour. Especially this green. Not bright or lime, but a soft, smoky green which complimented her natural colouring. She was wearing another skirt and top, obviously a fashion favourite with her. The skirt was darker than her top and was made of a floaty material. Softly gathered at the waist, it fell to her ankles and swished a little when she walked. The top had tight, three-quarter sleeves and a low crossover neckline which would have been criminal without a bra, yet still provocative with one. Her red-gold hair was back up, with lots of curls kissing her face and neck. The love bite he'd given her, he noted, seemed to have disappeared.

Make-up, he supposed.

Her make-up was, indeed, perfect, enhancing her already lovely complexion, eyes and mouth. Everything about her was perfect, including the sexy bronze slip-on sandals she was wearing, which had no backs and three-inch heels.

But the *coup de grâce* was her earrings.

Talk about exotic! Gold and dangling, they had a large heart covering each lobe from which fell gold chains of various lengths supporting either a gold star or a gold heart on the ends. They swung and tinkled together when she moved, a perversely erotic sight and sound.

Luke had watched her long slow walk down the stairs with almost hypnotised eyes. By the time she'd reached the bottom, his far from sated flesh had been in a right state.

Now, as he sat in his car, gripping the wheel tightly, he began to wonder if she'd deliberately made herself look extra sexy tonight. Though for what reason? A secret sadistic form of vengeance, or an outright attempt at seducing him? Had she really had that glass of wine she'd said she'd had? Or was that a ploy to be alone with him again at the end of the night?

To give her credit, she wasn't acting flirtatiously, but he doubted that would ever be Celia's way. Not that she needed to flirt. She just had to be breathing to affect a man.

Luke sucked in a deep breath himself, then wished he hadn't. Because the perfume she was wearing was as tantalising as the rest of her, especially in the confines of the car. It smelt of vanilla, and he'd always been partial to vanilla.

Frankly, Luke could not recall being this turned on in years. It was difficult to function, or focus on any other subject but sex. Was that what it had been like when his father had been with her mother? Had he found her so sexually irresistible that he'd forgotten everything else? His wife? His marriage vows? His normal sense of decency and honour?

Luke shook his head over the horrible thought that he was living some sort of ghastly replay of the past.

"Do you look much like your mother?" he asked abruptly.

She turned her head to face him but he kept *his* eyes on the road ahead.

"Quite a lot, I'm told," she said. "But I think she's much better looking than me. I'm a size larger. I'm also taller. And tougher," she added firmly.

Was that some kind of hint, her being tougher? Or was she just warning him to be gentle with her mother?

"We must be nearly there," he said.

"Turn right as soon as you get over this bridge. Then hard right again. The road follows the creek. Aunt Helen's house is a few hundred metres along it on the left. It's two-storeyed with a double garage out the front and a large porch. But I'll tell you when to stop."

"Do that."

"Stop," she commanded a couple of minutes later, and he pulled over in front of a cream brick house which was exactly as she'd described. A project home, he noted, but one with a sense of style, especially in the gabled roof.

Luke was not an architectural snob. He thought project-built homes had come a long way since the uninspiring three-bedroom boxes of the sixties. Not everyone, he appreciated, could afford individually designed homes.

"Aunt Helen's husband works for the local power station," Celia explained as they walked together towards the front porch. "He's working the four till midnight shift tonight so he won't be here. Aunt Helen does have three sons as well, but they're all grown-up and living away from home."

"Why are you telling me all this?" Luke asked warily, still not sure what she was up to.

"No reason. Just thought you might like to know the lie of the land," she added with a smile. A sweet smile. Almost a flirtatious one.

The only lie of the land Luke wanted to know at that moment, he decided ruefully, was hers. She was playing at something here and he didn't like the feel of it. Nor the smell of it, for that matter. That was a provocative perfume! He could almost taste it, the thought conjuring up visions of his doing just that. Tasting it. And tasting *her*. All over.

He sighed as he stepped up onto the front porch. It was going to be a long evening.

Concentrate on the mother and forget the daughter!

Yeah, right. As if that's going to help, he thought irritably. Dear old Dad did exactly the same to the mother as I want to do to the daughter. And he did it for twenty years!

Luke sighed again.

"Why are you sighing like that?" Celia said, pouncing, the sweet smile fading. "I thought this was what you wanted. To meet my mother."

"I do. Or I did. But the situation is a little different now. It's become awkward."

"I don't see how. It's not as though my mother knows anything about our relationship."

Warning bells went off in Luke's brain. "We don't *have* a relationship, Celia," he pointed out firmly. "We had sex together. Once. And there will be no repeat performance. You have my word on that."

When her pale cheeks went a guilty shade of pink, Luke knew the truth. She *had* been planning on seducing him.

Luke wasn't sure if the realisation aroused or angered him. Because if she was prepared to go to bed with him again, *knowing* he had a steady girlfriend back in Sydney, then she was just doing it for the sex. And he'd thought more of her than that.

Okay, so it must be tempting for her, wanting to experience what she'd experienced with him one more time. Orgasms had a way of being very addictive. And coinciding orgasms during sex were as rare as hen's teeth.

He'd never had a coinciding one with Isabel. If he

allowed for the fact that a lot of women faked them in order to flatter their lovers, then he had possibly never had one. And yes, it had been out of this world, pleasurewise.

But that was still no excuse, in Luke's opinion. If he could resist temptation, then she could as well.

"I would have thought you'd be the last girl on earth who would tolerate a two-timing lover," he said harshly.

"I don't know what you're talking about," she said, and pushed the front doorbell.

"Oh, yes, you do, sweetheart," he hissed under his breath. "You know exactly what I'm talking about. Don't try to play me for a fool. I suspected the moment you sashayed downstairs in that sexy outfit that you had a hidden agenda for tonight. That, and that pathetic excuse about the wine. You didn't have any extra glass. You just wanted me to drive you here and then drive you home. Alone. You want another sample of what I gave you this afternoon. Why don't you admit it, instead of pulling this innocent act?"

Celia could feel her face going red.

"And to think I believed all that holier than thou crap about you not wanting me to touch you again!" he raged on. "The truth is you *do* want me to touch you again. You want me to touch you again one hell of a lot!"

Celia had never felt such shame, nor such outrage. He was right, but he was so wrong. She didn't want just what he'd given her this afternoon. She wanted so much more. She wanted what he'd said they didn't have: a real relationship. Or the chance of one.

She was trying to find the words to tell him exactly that when the front door opened and there stood Aunt Helen, looking her usual smart self in black trousers and an embroidered red top. Her once long auburn tresses—now worn short and died blond—showed evidence of her regular Friday trip to the hairdresser with not a hair out of place. She was not as striking as her kid sister, but still very attractive for her fifty-three years.

"Hello, Auntie," Celia said, struggling to find a smile through her emotional distress. "Sorry we're a bit late. This is Luke. Luke, my Aunt Helen."

He didn't seem to have any trouble smiling, nor in charming her aunt with a kiss on the cheek and a few well chosen words.

"Oh, my," her aunt said, looking a bit shell-shocked as she led them both inside and straight into the open-plan lounge. The house had no hallway as such, with the stairs leading to the upper floor on the left of the front door. "Celia was right. You do look a lot like your father. Not that I ever met him. But I've seen a couple of photos. Now, why don't you sit down in here with me, Luke, while Celia runs upstairs and talks to her mother. I popped a casserole in the oven for dinner, so we can have that any time you're ready, Celia. I'm not sure Jessica will join us for the meal," she said, directing her words at Luke. "She's not eating much at the moment. Hopefully, your visit might perk her up. Meanwhile, I've prepared a plate of nibbles for us and opened a nice bottle of Hunter Valley red. You like red wine, Luke?''

"Love it," he said as he sat down on the floral sofa. "But I'm driving, so I can only have a glass or two, then I'll have to swap to water."

Aunt Helen beamed approval at him as she settled into one of the matching armchairs. "Sensible man. Nothing worse than people who drink and drive. So irresponsible. They cause so many accidents."

Celia winced. "Aunt Helen," she said in sharp warning and her aunt glanced her way, her expression bewildered.

"Luke's parents," Celia said softly.

Her aunt looked stricken. "Oh, dear. Oh, how stupid of me. Luke, I'm so sorry. I just didn't think."

"It's all right, Helen. Truly. I know you meant no harm. Besides, better to talk about something out in the open than to pretend it never happened. Which is one of the reasons I've come here tonight. To find some answers for what happened between my father and your sister."

"What kind of answers? The simple truth is your father had an extramarital affair with my sister. For twenty years. I'm afraid there are no mysteries about it, Luke."

"That may be, but the thing is, Helen, I always believed my father was the perfect family man. Other people did too. Of course, I know no one's perfect. I'm not that naive. But I can't accept the image of my father as a heartless womaniser. It doesn't ring true. Since I can't ask him for some answers in person, I was hoping your sister could shed some more light on the subject, so I too can come to terms with what he did. My mother, thank goodness, will never now know what happened. But I do. And I—''

Luke suddenly broke off and stared, not at Celia, who was still standing, but at something just over her shoulder. Celia knew instinctively what he'd seen. Oh, dear, she thought, her heart sinking as she turned.

Her mother was coming slowly down the stairs, her eyes wide, one hand at her throat, the other clutching the banisters. She was wearing a dusky pink dressing-gown, sashed at the waist, pink satin slippers and not a scrap of make-up.

But for all that, in the soft evening light, she looked so exquisitely beautiful, it was heart-breaking. There was a light hanging high above her head, casting a golden glow over her hair which was fluffed out over her very slender shoulders. She'd lost considerable weight since her lover's death, making her already large green eyes look larger. The dark rings underneath them were not unattractive, only adding to her haunting beauty. She looked like a character from one of those old melodramatic movies: the beautiful but mad bride who'd been locked up in a tower for years but who sometimes escaped in the dead of night.

''It's Luke,'' Celia said straight away before her mother got the wrong idea over whom she was seeing. ''Lionel's son. He's come to visit and he has some good news for you.''

Her mother's bewildered eyes briefly shifted to Celia before returning to Luke.

"I...I heard Lionel's voice," she choked out. "And I thought...I thought I was going insane." Tears filled her eyes but she didn't cry. She descended the last few steps very slowly, as though sleep-walking, then equally slowly came forward, staring at Luke all the while. "You're so like him," she murmured dazedly. "You sound like him. Look like him."

Luke rose and took her hands in his, drawing her over to the lounge. "So I'm told, ma'am," he said gently as they sat down together. "And your daughter, if I might say so, is startlingly like you."

"What? Oh, yes, people say that all the time. But close family don't always see the similarities, do they?"

"True."

Celia exchanged glances with her aunt who suggested with her eyes that they leave the room. But Celia was reluctant to do so. What if her mother got upset? What if Luke said the wrong thing?

She frowned and shook her head, so they remained, standing guard over their fragile charge. Celia began to worry that she hadn't thought this meeting through properly. All she'd been thinking about, in the end, was herself.

When Jessica reached out to touch Luke's arm Celia stiffened. Her mother was a toucher, but not everyone liked that kind of thing. But Luke didn't pull away, for which Celia was grateful.

"How did you find out about me?" Jessica asked in puzzled tones.

Celia tensed up again. What would Luke tell her? Not

the whole truth, surely. She tried to catch his eye but he seemed determined not to look at her.

"Dad went to see his solicitor the day before he died," he began, "and told him about you in confidence. You see, he wanted to gift over the house at Pretty Point to you. Unfortunately, the accident happened before he could do that, so the solicitor referred the matter to me. Your relationship wasn't spelt out in black and white but I suspected you had to be more than good friends for Dad to want to give you such an expensive property. So I drove up here today and, by coincidence, Celia was at the house when I arrived."

Celia flinched when her mother threw her a questioning glance.

"I needed a place to spend a quiet weekend," she said. "Somewhere I could just rest and read."

Luke finally looked at her—his eyes wry—and Celia struggled not to blush.

"But I still wanted to be close to you," she added. "I didn't think anyone would mind. No one was living there and it needed a dust through, anyway."

"But I thought you hated the place," her mother said, frowning.

Celia sighed. "Not the house itself, Mum," she muttered. Just what went on in it.

Luke shot her a sharp glance as if reading her mind and warning her to remain discreetly silent.

"As I was saying," he said, jumping in, "when Celia answered the door, I thought at first that she was the Ms Gilbert the solicitor told me about."

Celia flinched and closed her eyes. Oh, no. Don't tell

her what I did. Oh, please, don't do that! That would be much worse than anything I might have said just now.

"Celia quickly explained she wasn't my father's…er…friend," he continued rather delicately. "Her mother was. By then, I knew you and he had to have been lovers. Seeing the house was very telling. I know his personal style well. He built that place especially for you two, didn't he?"

She nodded, her eyes flooding anew. "You…you must hate me," she choked out, two big tears running down her cheeks.

Luke covered her hands with his own in what Celia thought was an awfully kind gesture. A lump formed in her throat, tears of her own threatening. He really was a very nice man.

Luke shook his head. "No," he said. "What point would there be in my hating you? I can see you're not some kind of ruthless home-wrecker or money-grubbing gold digger. You're a very nice lady. And I'm sure my father cared for you very much."

It was heart-breaking, the look of desperate hope that filled her mother's face. Celia understood that kind of desperation now.

"You…you really think so?" Jessica said shakily.

Celia held her breath as she awaited Luke's reply.

"I'm sure of it," he pronounced, and she almost burst into tears of relief and gratitude. "My father was a good man. A decent man. The only thing which would make him be unfaithful to my mother for twenty years was the deepest of affections. I just want to know why, if he wasn't happy with my mother—and he clearly couldn't have been—why he didn't divorce her and marry you?''

Jessica glanced worriedly at her sister and daughter before looking back at her lover's son. ''Your father...he...he told me things in confidence. Things about your mother, Luke. Things he didn't really want other people to know.''

''I see. But my father's gone now, and so is my mother. I really need to know this, ma'am. I need some answers. My mother...was she...frigid?'' Luke asked reluctantly. ''Was that it?''

''In a fashion,'' Jessica hedged, then sighed. ''I guess there's no point in not telling you. It's not as though anyone in this room will tell anyone else, will they?''

''Of course not,'' both Celia and Aunt Helen murmured in unison.

''Tell me,'' Luke prodded softly. ''Please.''

''Your mother was attacked as a young girl.''

Luke sucked in sharply. ''Raped, you mean?''

''Yes. By a gang of louts. She was thirteen at the time.''

Celia was horrified. The poor girl. And poor Luke. He was looking poleaxed.

''She never told anyone,'' her mother went on. ''She kept it a secret. She pretended it never happened. But of course, you can't do that, can you, and stay mentally and emotionally healthy?''

''I wouldn't think so,'' Luke murmured sadly.

''Lionel thought she was a virgin when he married her because she wouldn't let him touch her before the wedding. As you can imagine, the wedding night wasn't a huge success. Neither was the honeymoon. Lionel said she tried so hard to please him yet was obviously hating everything about sex. He said he loved her but nothing he did made things better. He was actually thinking about divorce when she fell pregnant with you, Luke. Naturally, he couldn't leave her then.

"After you were born, she went into a deep postnatal depression which lasted over a year and eventually she became quite manic. Some days she'd be angry and argumentative, on others withdrawn and silent. Sex was a minefield best left totally alone. When Lionel came home one day and found her screaming at you in your cot for being a boy, and that all boys grew up to be bad, he took her straight to a psychiatrist. Under hypnotherapy, the truth finally came out. After extensive counselling and medication, she surprised Lionel by becoming an almost perfect wife and mother, although she never did get any pleasure from sex. Yet if Lionel didn't regularly sleep with her she'd become tearful and suspicious. Lionel said it nearly killed him to see how relieved she'd be when he had to go away, for whatever reason, because that meant no sex for a while."

Celia could see Luke was struggling with the impact of these appalling revelations, his face mirroring both distress and disbelief. On her part, she wasn't sure what to believe. Surely Lionel couldn't have invented this horror story to excuse his actions in his mistress's eyes. That would have been really evil.

"I still don't understand why he didn't divorce Mum after meeting you," Luke said, frowning. "I mean, from the sounds of things, my mother would probably have been relieved.''

Jessica gave him an odd look. ''You mean you haven't figured that out yet?''

''Sorry. I'm not sure what you mean.''

''The reason Lionel didn't leave your mother for me was because of you, Luke.''

''*Me?*''

''Yes, you. Believe me when I say your father loved you far more than he loved either your mother or me. Far, far more! Your happiness and security were his number one priorities. Everything was to be sacrificed for you, Luke. And it was.''

CHAPTER NINE

LUKE was stunned.

Jessica reached out and patted his arm. "Did your father ever tell you that his own father left his mother for another woman when he was just a boy?"

"No! He...he said his father died of a heart attack when he was ten and his mother when he was twenty. Of some kind of liver failure. He said she'd been ill for years. She'd caught some kind of virus."

"His father did die of a heart attack, but only recently. Your grandfather had contacted your father when he became ill, but Lionel would have nothing to do with him. He said to me that his father had been dead in his mind for over forty years. His mother—your grandmother—did die when Lionel was twenty. That wasn't a lie. And yes, of liver failure. But not because of a virus. She became an alcoholic after her husband left and eventually drank herself to death."

Luke shook his head, shocked, not only by these new revelations but the extent of this woman's knowledge.

"Why didn't Dad tell *me* any of this?" he demanded, feeling frustrated and almost angry that he'd been kept so much in the dark about his family history. He could understand why he hadn't been told about his mother's wretched past, but why keep his grandfather's actions—

and existence—a secret? And why lie over how his grandmother had died?

Just how many lies *had* his father fed him over the years?

"Lionel wouldn't have wanted you to know because he was ashamed," his mistress confessed. "Of both his parents. His father's desertion had hurt him terribly. That was why he couldn't leave your mother after you were born. Because he could never do to his son what his father had done to him. He explained that to me right from the beginning and I understood. I really did."

Maybe she did. But Luke didn't. Yes, he could understand his father making such a sacrifice for him during his vulnerable growing-up years. But what about after he'd grown up and left home? What about during the years he'd spent overseas? What was his father's excuse then?

No, no, Luke hated to admit it but this poor woman was the victim of male selfishness. She'd become a convenience by then. A beautiful, sexy, soft-hearted woman who was prepared to give his dad what his poor emotionally damaged mother hadn't been capable of.

In short, she'd been used.

Luke was more ashamed of his father at that moment than he'd been since finding out about his extramarital affair. To have a bit of sex on the side was forgiveable under the circumstances of his marriage. To put his son first whilst he'd been a mere boy was also forgiveable. But to string this lovely lady along for twenty years was *not* forgiveable.

Something of what he was feeling must have shown on his face because Celia's mother suddenly looked sad.

"I know what you're thinking," she said. "Why didn't he leave your mother after you finished university and went overseas to live? It wouldn't have affected you that badly by then."

"That thought did occur to me," Luke confessed reluctantly.

She shrugged her terribly thin shoulders. "Not as often as it's occurred to me, but by then I wasn't brave enough to ask. Perhaps Lionel thought it was too late to make such a big change in his life. Perhaps your good opinion of him still mattered more than I did. But I suspect he just couldn't bear to break your poor mother's heart. I do know he compromised a bit by building that house for us and by spending more time with me. He used to tell your mother he was going fishing for the weekend and she seemed to believe him."

Luke nodded. "She would have. He's been going fishing all his life."

"Actually, no. Most times he said he was going fishing during the last twenty years, he was coming to see me. There used to be an old fishing cabin at Pretty Point where we'd meet. But it eventually got vandalised and was partially burned down."

Luke realised somewhat bitterly why his father had been so understanding about his no longer wanting to go fishing at Pretty Point. That had been when he'd turned twelve, exactly twenty years ago, the same year he'd met Ms Jessica Gilbert.

Luke looked at her and thought how breathtakingly beautiful she must have been back then. She was still very beautiful…

"I want to apologise for my father," he said, and meant it. "I don't think he treated you very well. Or fairly. And I think he knew it too. I'm sure his wanting to gift you the property at Pretty Point was his way of saying sorry, so of course you must have it. I've already told Celia that I will see to the deed being transferred to you."

Luke was moved by the emotion in her eyes. "You'd do that for me?"

"It's what my father wanted."

"Oh…oh, dear…" She dissolved into tears then and he could do nothing but take her into his arms and try to comfort her. A piece of cake, compared to taking her daughter into his arms.

"There, there," he soothed, stroking her hair and back. "Please don't cry."

"Lionel always hated me to cry," she sobbed.

No doubt, Luke thought ruefully. And I bet you cried often, you poor thing. It was wicked, what he did to you. Wicked. He should have walked away and let you find a decent life for yourself, with a man who could have given you a darned sight more than the occasional weekend. Whatever had possessed him?

Luke glanced over Jessica's shoulder to her even more beautiful daughter, and knew exactly what had possessed him.

A powerful force, physical passion. Especially in a man.

Luke vowed not to let his passion for Celia sway his good judgement. Come the end of this evening, he was out of here, never to return. But, while he had the chance, he was going to put this poor woman back on the path to some kind of future happiness, because the last thing he wanted on his conscience was Celia's mother topping herself.

"Why don't you take your mum upstairs to get dressed for dinner?" Luke directed at Celia. "You need to eat, Jessica," he added with a firm glance into her still teary eyes. "And to talk. We'll have a good chinwag about Dad, shall we? You can tear strips off the old man, if you want to. And we'll down a couple of glasses of Helen's excellent wine. Shall we say ten minutes to dinner? You could manage that, Helen?"

Helen smiled at him. "No trouble."

"Good. Hop to it then, Celia. And for pity's sake, don't take as long as *you* did to get ready tonight. After ten minutes, I'll be coming up there to drag the pair of you downstairs personally."

Celia bristled, but then relented. Because he was right. This was exactly what her mother needed to do. To pull herself together and to talk about Lionel. To demythologise the man whom she'd falsely idolised. To have a proper wake for him, so to speak.

Then she might begin the healing process.

Celia hurried forward and led her somewhat dazed mother upstairs, plonking her down on the guest bed whilst she rustled up some clothes. She found a pair of stretchy blue jeans and a white cashmere sweater, neither of which needed ironing.

"Here, Mum. Put these on."

"He's remarkable, isn't he?" her mother said a bit dreamily as she did as her daughter ordered. "Just like Lionel."

Celia rolled her eyes. Her mother was such a romantic. It pained Celia to think she was more like her than she'd ever realised.

"He looks just like Lionel too," her mother added as she walked over to the dressing table and picked up her hair brush. "And he's just as forceful. There's something about a forceful man that's hard to resist, don't you think?"

Celia tried not to think of the way Luke had ordered her to undress this afternoon. Because thinking about such things made her want him to do the same again. And that just wasn't going to happen. Luke had been equally forceful on that score out at the front door.

"Have I time to put some lipstick and perfume on?" Jessica asked.

"If you're quick."

"What about my hair? I should really put it up. It's a mess."

"I don't think we've got the time for that."

"It won't take me long." And it didn't, her mother winding her hair around in her hands a couple of times and anchoring it in seconds with a few pins. "There. See? I was quick. Come on, let's get going. I want to talk to Luke some more. And *look* at him some more."

Don't we all, Celia thought ruefully as she followed in her mother's surprisingly brisk step.

The dinner was a great success, if her mother's

emerging good spirits were the basis for judgement. Luke was patience personified. And Aunt Helen looked very pleased with how things had turned out.

But Celia found the whole thing a trial. Just looking at Luke made her even more depressed inside, as did listening to her mother recount all the intimate little details she knew about Luke's life, things Lionel had told her over the years. Mostly his son's triumphs, both sportwise and academically.

Over the couple of hours she spent sitting at the dining table, Celia learned Luke had been captain of the basketball team, captain of the debating team, captain of his school of course. Luke, the youth, had been nothing short of an all round star! He'd won numerous awards during his university days as well, one being a rarely given scholarship to further his studies overseas, the architectural equivalent of being a Rhodians scholar.

At twenty-two, he'd jetted off for London, where he'd stayed on after finishing his studies, gaining invaluable experience by working for a highly prestigious international company that had offices in Paris, Rome and New York. All in all, Luke had stayed overseas for nearly eight years. When he'd returned two years ago he'd entered a competition to design a retirement village and had won. The prize had been a great wad of cash plus a lucrative contract to work for the architectural company that had sponsored the prize. He'd been working there ever since.

Aside from details of Luke's career, Celia also learned of several other personal crises in his growing-up years, in particular his breaking his leg during abseiling at a scout camp, thereby missing out on trying out for the Australian schoolboy basketball team—clearly considered a disaster at the time.

Luke now laughed about it, saying time put everything into perspective.

By the time coffee was served around nine-thirty, Celia realised Lionel hadn't exactly been demythologised during all this. He'd come across as a doting father who'd taken great pride in his quite remarkable son. Even worse was the realisation her own mother sounded just as proud of Luke, almost as though *she* were his mother.

Celia felt quite jealous.

"You know, Luke," her mother started up again as they all sipped their coffee, "your father was extremely relieved when you finally came back to live and work in Australia. He was worried you might meet some girl overseas and stay there for ever. He was over the moon when you became engaged to a Sydney girl."

Celia's coffee cup froze at her lips. *Engaged?* Had her mother just said *engaged*?

Her eyes went to his but he refused to meet them.

"If I recall rightly," Jessica said, sweeping on, oblivious to her daughter's stunned reaction, "your wedding is very soon. Unless you've decided to call it off after the accident, that is," she added a bit worriedly when she noted Luke's rather grim expression.

"No," he said. "No, the wedding's definitely going ahead, a fortnight tomorrow, as planned. I did think of postponing the ceremony for a while but, in the end, I decided nothing would be served by that. Isabel's parents had spent a lot of time and money organising everything, and I didn't think it would be fair on them. Or on Isabel, for that matter.''

Celia's knuckles whitened as her fingers tightened around her coffee cup.

''Your father wouldn't have wanted you to postpone anything,'' Jessica reassured him. ''He was very keen on your getting married, *and* on your Isabel. I hear she's very beautiful.''

''Yes,'' Luke agreed. ''Isabel's a lovely looking girl. And a lovely person as well.''

Now his eyes did go to Celia's. And she saw a wealth of apology in them. Yet no guilt. Amazing! No guilt!

She could barely believe it.

Luke was engaged! And the wedding was in a fortnight's time! Yet today, he'd been making love to *her*.

No, no, of course he hadn't been making love to her, Celia amended bitterly in her mind. He'd just been screwing her. That's all the Freeman men ever did to the Gilbert girls. Screw them.

Her coffee cup clattered back down into the saucer as a cold fury invaded her heart, and her eyes.

Luke put down his coffee cup as well, his own eyes closing briefly before opening again. When they did, they were quite unreadable.

''Speaking of the wedding has reminded me that I have a lot to do this weekend,'' he said in a flat but firm voice. ''So if you'll excuse me, ladies, I really do have to be going. Celia? Are you ready to go?''

''Any time you are,'' she replied through gritted teeth.

"You'll come back to visit some time, won't you?" her mother asked him plaintively.

"Actually, no, Jessica. I won't. Not personally. My solicitor will be in touch, however. I'm very glad to have met you and talked with you, and I do wish you all the best for the future, but I think it wise to leave it at this one time."

Her mother looked crestfallen, but resigned. She nodded. "I can appreciate your feelings. It must have been a big shock for you, finding out about me. But you've been very decent about it all. And very kind. Let me just say how very sorry I am if what we did hurt you, but at least your mother never found out. And I did love your father very very much."

When Luke stood up, walked round and bent to kiss her mother on the cheek, it took all of Celia's will-power not to jump up and scream all sorts of verbal abuse at him.

Only the thought of her mother's emotional health held her back. If Celia said anything at all about what Luke had done to her this afternoon, it might undo all the good he'd done here tonight.

He wasn't all bad, she conceded, just as Lionel hadn't been all bad. But both father and son had been unfaithful to the women they were supposedly committed to. And in doing so, they'd left a trail of emotional wreckage behind them.

Celia knew it would be a long, long time before she got over Luke Freeman. Maybe even longer than it would take her mother to get over Luke's father. Because Lionel was dead now, and Luke was very much alive. Celia had to live with the daily reality from now on that, somewhere in Sydney, Luke would be living with the lovely Isabel, married to her, making love to her, having children with her. Whilst she would be alone, alone with her regrets and her heartache.

CHAPTER TEN

"SAY something, for pity's sake," Luke ground out.

Celia glanced over at him, then turned and opened the passenger door. During the fifteen minutes it had taken for them to make their farewells and drive in total silence back to Pretty Point, her need for an angry confrontation with him had disintegrated. What would be the point? What would it achieve?

Without a word, she swung her feet out of his car and onto the gravel drive.

"I didn't tell you I was engaged to Isabel because I didn't want to hurt you any further," he threw after her in a pained voice. "You have to believe me, Celia."

Now she did turn to look at him. "Why must I believe you, Luke? Because it will make *you* feel better? You're a coward, just like your father."

"I'm no coward," he grated out. "And neither was my father. I've been thinking some more about what your mother said and I was wrong to condemn him. You were, too."

"Oh, come on. I had every right to condemn him!"

"No, be fair, Celia. Put yourself in my father's position. Whose happiness would you have chosen? He did what he thought he had to do. He put my happiness before his and, in the end, my mother's as well. He knew she couldn't have coped with his leaving her after all those years of marriage.''

"And what about *my* mother?" Celia said, lashing out. "Do you think she coped? You saw her. Your father nearly destroyed her."

"He should have walked away right from the start, yes. But that would have been extremely difficult, under the circumstances. And your mother knew what she was getting into. She knew he was married after that first night and she kept on seeing him. She'll bounce back, your mum. She's tougher than you think."

"And what about me?" she threw at him. "Do you think I'll bounce back after this?"

"You told me you were tougher than your mother," he reminded her.

Tears welled up in her eyes. "Well, I'm not. I—I—Oh, just go! Go and marry your lovely Isabel. But I hope she knows what she's getting. A man who doesn't love her as she probably deserves to be loved. A man who just two weeks before his wedding forgot she even existed. Tell me, Luke, have you ever felt with Isabel what you felt with me this afternoon?"

He didn't say a single word, but his face told it all.

"No," she said, sneering. "My betting is you'll be back too, just like your father. At least he had some excuse. What's yours, Luke? You're not even married yet. You should do the honorable thing and call your wedding off."

His eyes looked haunted. "You can't expect me to give up the substance for the shadow. I've only known you a few short hours. This thing between us—it—it won't last.''

''It lasted twenty years between our parents,'' she pointed out savagely.

''It lasted because they had an affair! They had all the excitement and the sex, and none of the mundane. They might not have been so happy if they'd married. It's hard to find happiness over the misery of others.''

''I hope you remember that.''

''You'll get over me.''

''I won't,'' she declared, and he stared at her in alarm.

''I've fallen in love with you, Luke Freeman. Oh, I know you think love can't happen as quickly as that. But it has, and nothing you say will change it. I love you. I love you. I love you!''

''Don't keep saying that.'' He groaned.

''Why? Because once again you don't want to hear it? You *are* a coward, Luke Freeman. A miserable coward. You don't deserve my love. You don't deserve any woman's love. I feel sorry for poor Isabel because she's going to be awfully short-changed in your marriage. I wonder how many nights you'll lie in bed with her, thinking of me, before you come crawling back up here, wanting another sample of the magic we shared today.''

''After I marry Isabel, I won't be back,'' he bit out. ''And that's a promise.''

''You'd better not because, let me warn you, if you do, I'll bring you down. With my love, and with my hate. Oh, yes, Luke. I'm not totally like my mother. I'm not nearly so sweet or forgiving. If you ever show up in my life again, I won't settle for just your body. I won't settle for anything less than your very soul. And once that's mine, you'll be the one who's destroyed. You have my promise on that!''

His face grew dark and his finger jabbed white hot fury at her. ''This is the very reason why I won't ever be back. Because I can't stand this sort of thing. I want peace in my life, not some crazy woman telling me she loves me one minute, then threatening me the next. You think you love me? Well, you don't. If you did, you'd have some compassion for me. Have you any idea what I've gone through these past two weeks? Sheer and utter hell! My parents killed and nobody to bury them but me. Can you imagine what it's like to choose coffins for both your parents? Choose the clothes they will wear for their funerals? Make all those awful decisions which have to be made? And then the funerals themselves, all the while trying not to break down, because men aren't expected to cry, are they?''

Celia stared at him in horror as his eyes actually glistened.

''But,'' he choked out, ''I've felt like crying. I still feel like crying when I think about it all. My parents...both gone. In a heartbeat. And then what happens? I discover that my beloved father, my hero, wasn't such a hero after all. Can you imagine how I felt when I found out he had feet of clay? How I felt when you answered the door today and I thought *you* were my father's mistress? A girl young enough to be his daughter. Yet you didn't tell me the truth, did you? Oh, no. You had your own private, vengeful agenda, Celia

Gilbert, and Luke Freeman's feelings didn't count. You deliberately let me think my father had been the worst kind of sexual predator.''

Remorse ripped through Celia as the reality of what she'd put Luke through hit home hard. ''Luke, I—I'm sorry. Truly. I was just trying to—''

''Protect your mother,'' he finished bitterly. ''Well, it's a pity you didn't think what results your charade might produce. Because no sooner had I started thinking of you as my father's mistress, than I started wanting you as my own. I was well on the slippery slide to hell long before you started crying and I took you in my arms. I'm in hell now, still wanting you so badly it's killing me. But it's not love driving me, sweetheart. It's lust. Pure, animal lust. At least *I* know the difference.

''So what am I to do, Celia? You tell me. Walk away like I've been trying to do? Or go with you back inside my father's decadent little love nest and take you to hell with me? You choose, darling. You choose.''

She stared at him, heart pounding, eyes widening. ''What do you mean? Take me to hell with you...''

''I mean just that. I still want you, in all the ways I've been thinking of having you from our first meeting. I don't love you and I won't pretend I do. You want my soul? It's yours, along with my body. Take it if you want it, because I'm tired of trying to do what's right. I'm tired of everything.''

Celia heard the torment in his voice and her heart filled with a sweet longing to comfort him, to take him in her arms and make him see that it wasn't just lust driving him. He *could* love her, if only he'd let himself.

He didn't love this Isabel. Luke wasn't the type of man to be unfaithful to a woman he truly loved. Surely he would see that, in time.

But she didn't have much time, did she?

"When do you have to be back in Sydney?" she asked abruptly.

"What's that got to do with anything?" he snapped.

"You said you didn't have a date with Isabel tonight. What about tomorrow night?"

"She's not expecting me back till the end of the weekend. She thinks I'm up here, revisiting my childhood past and getting in touch with my father's spirit. What a joke!"

"I don't think it's a joke at all," Celia murmured. "That's exactly what you've been doing."

He laughed. An awful sound. "I'm sure Dad's very proud of me for following in his footsteps to a T. Come on. Let's go inside and go to bed. That *is* what you want, isn't it?" He looked straight at her with a challenging gaze, his black eyes still glittering.

No, she thought despairingly. Not like this.

But if she sent him away...

She had one weekend, one weekend to make him see they were meant for each other.

"Yes," she agreed a bit shakily, knowing the risk she was taking but compelled just the same.

"And you don't want me to leave in the morning, do you? You want me to stay here with you all weekend."

"Yes," she said, more firmly this time.

"I thought so. Just don't go telling me how you love me all the time. I don't need any more romantic bulldust, or any more guilt trips. I don't need anything this weekend but you, naked and willing. Do you think you could manage that?''

Luke turned away from the hurt look on her face and climbed out of the car, slamming the door behind him. He knew he was being cruel. And he hated himself for it. But he also couldn't seem to stop.

In the space of one miserable day she'd turned his life upside down, and had made him do things he'd thought he'd never do. He was still doing them!

When he reached her side of the car, she was standing there, calmly waiting for him, no longer looking hurt, just breathtakingly beautiful in the moonlight. His flesh leapt at the sight of her and he abandoned all hope of resisting temptation.

''Why did I have to meet you now?'' He groaned frustratedly as he pulled her into his arms. ''And why did you have to be this beautiful?''

He didn't expect an answer, because he was already kissing her before she could do more than part her perfect lips.

His tongue met hers and they both moaned. His arms tightened around her and the urge to make love to her, then and there, was intense.

His need triggered an unwanted memory and his mouth burst up from hers. ''Damn and blast. I don't have any more condoms with me. Do you?''

She stared up at him with a desperation that must have reflected his own.

''No. But you—you—'' She broke off, her expression anguished.

"But I what?"

"You don't really need them. Not unless you think you do. I'm a regular blood donor. And I haven't been with anyone for months."

"Well, I'm no risk. You have my word on that. What about pregnancy?"

"No chance of that this weekend."

He looked at her and thought that a man would be crazy to trust a woman who claimed she loved him. But strangely, he *did* trust her.

Or did he just *want* to trust her? Had his normally careful character been corrupted by the thought of making love to her all weekend without having to worry about using protection, of staying inside her afterwards till he was ready to do it again. And again. And again.

The prospect of such pleasures was simply too much. "Fine," he bit out, grabbing her nearest hand and pulling her towards the house. "Come on before common sense returns and I change my mind."

He almost laughed at the hypocrisy of that last statement. Nothing was going to change his mind. Nothing was going to stop him, short of a bomb falling on top of them both.

He reached for where he'd seen her hide the key on a ledge and jammed it into the lock. "I trust you're not going to change *your* mind at the last moment?" he asked as he threw open the door.

"No," she said, her green eyes glittering wildly, her breasts rising and falling under her green top. She was as excited as he was, he realised. Too excited, perhaps, to think clearly.

Was this the kind of passion their parents had shared? If it was, then it explained a lot. His father's deceptions. Her mother's ongoing willingness to be used.

"You know you shouldn't always be so quick to take a man's word," he muttered. "Like you said earlier today, men lie to get sex, and they'd lie a lot to get what you're offering."

"You're not that kind of liar," she said with such confidence that he was momentarily rattled.

"You called me a coward a minute ago," he reminded her, pulling her inside and kicking the door shut behind them.

"I was angry with you."

"And you're not any more?" He pressed her up against the door, his erection almost at bursting point.

"I understand you better now."

He shook his head. "Well, I don't understand you, Celia Gilbert. And I don't want to. I just want to…"

"Take me to hell with you," she finished for him before he could say the crude word that had sprung to his lips.

"That's it, precisely."

"Impossible. Because I'm going to take you to heaven first." His breath caught when she snaked her arms up around his neck and reached up on tiptoe. "And I'm going to keep you there," she whispered huskily against his mouth, "all weekend long."

CHAPTER ELEVEN

CELIA woke to the sun streaming into the room and Luke still fast asleep next to her. Quietly she levered herself up on one elbow and stared down at him, her heart contracting as the memories flooded back, not just of the night before, but the whole of yesterday.

In a way, it all seemed unreal. Like a dream. Or a nightmare.

Luke's naked body sprawled on top of the bed beside her, however, was very real. As were the feelings just looking at it evoked within her.

She wanted to reach out and touch him again. Stroke him. Stir him. She wanted to make his flesh grow hard and huge once more so that she could straddle him and ride him one more amazing time.

Was that love? she now wondered. Wanting to do that?

Or was it just lust? as Luke had insisted.

The female psyche, Celia conceded, was geared to love, to seeing all relationships with romantic, rose-coloured glasses.

There'd been nothing remotely romantic in their first torrid encounter up against the door last night. Nor their second, on the rug, in front of the fireplace.

Basic was the word that came to mind.

But afterwards, Luke had been very tender with her,

apologising for his roughness as he'd carried her up-stairs. Not that she'd really minded at the time. She'd been right there with him. As wildly excited as he'd been.

But she preferred the gentler lover he'd become once his first mad bursts of passion had been sated. She'd loved the way he'd washed her in the shower, kissing and caressing her all the while. And the way he'd dried her. So softly, yet sensually.

But nothing could compare with what he'd done to her when he'd carried her back to the bed. She'd vowed to take him to heaven, yet she'd been the one in heaven, with his mouth on her down there. She'd come so many times she lost count, till she'd begged him to stop.

He'd laughed, then had slid up her body and had eased himself back into her, bending her knees right back and hooking her ankles over his shoulders. She'd stared dazedly up at him as he'd rocked into her with a slow, voluptuous rhythm, his handsome face a study of intense concentration till eventually she'd begun moving with him, her hips lifting off the bed, her inner muscles squeezing him tight. He'd groaned then, and she'd known he'd been right on the edge. One more squeeze and he'd tipped right over.

She'd never watched a man come before. Not like that. She'd found it incredibly exciting, not minding at all that she hadn't come herself on that occasion.

"Witch," he'd called her afterwards, but smilingly. "Any more wine in that fridge downstairs?"

He'd brought a bottle of classic dry white back to bed and they'd drunk it together—straight from the bottle—and had talked and had laughed whilst she'd touched him and had kissed him, more and more intimately. She hadn't been able to help herself.

Of course, he hadn't minded. He hadn't minded at all. And before she'd known it she'd been on top of him and riding him, her nakedness on display for his eyes and hands, her earrings swinging back and forth with her rhythm. Once, he'd splashed some wine on her breasts and pulled her down so that he could lick it off. And when the wine had all gone, he'd rubbed the tip of the bottle against her till she'd splintered apart.

At the time, it had seemed so dizzyingly exciting.

Now, she didn't like to think about it.

Yet she had to think about it, didn't she? She had to think about the sort of woman she became when she was in bed with Luke: an uninhibited and wild creature who didn't seem to mind what he did to her, and whose ability to orgasm had increased a thousandfold.

Celia conceded it would be very easy to become addicted to having Luke as her lover, whether she was in love with him or not.

She believed her mother had fallen victim to a similar addiction with Luke's father, and that was why she'd never been able to break up with him. Lionel had been like a drug to her.

Celia couldn't bear the thought of ending up like her mother. And she might. She very well might, if Luke still married Isabel. And he'd given no indication as yet that he wouldn't.

Would she have the will-power to say no if he wanted her as *his* mistress? Would she send him away, or would she succumb, and keep stupidly hoping that he'd leave Isabel for her?

No. No. She couldn't do that to herself. She had to stop this right now!

Reefing her eyes away from Luke's magnificent male body she swung her legs over the side of the bed. The sound of her earrings tinkling had her reaching up and taking them off. Quietly, she slipped them into the top of the drawer of the bedside table. Best not wear *them* today. Luke had admitted during the night he found them an incredible turn-on and the last thing she wanted was to tempt Luke today. She just wanted to talk to him.

Celia sucked in a fortifying breath as she glanced at the bedside clock. It was just after ten.

Get up, she ordered herself. Get up. Get dressed, and go downstairs.

"And where do you think you're going?" Luke growled, snaking a long strong arm around her waist and pulling her back against him. His mouth nuzzled into her neck and his right hand homed in on a still sensitised breast.

Celia smothered a moan of pleasure. But, oh...he knew just what she liked. Or had learned to like during the night before. He'd been quite a teacher.

"I—I have to get up," she said, trying to ignore the exquisite sensation of his tugging on her nipple.

"Not yet," he said thickly, and angled his body to curl around hers.

When she felt his erection nudging between her legs, Celia stiffened.

No, don't think about how it feels when he's inside you, she told herself despairingly. Stop him, for pity's sake. Stop him!

She made some effort to struggle free and he grunted.

"All right. Not so impatient."

She gasped when he slipped inside her.

"There. That better?"

He thought she'd been wriggling with frustration!

She wanted to cry. Instead, she moaned. It felt so good, so very, very good.

He started pulsing into her with short, rapid strokes and soon she was making whimpering little sounds, deep in her throat.

"You like that?" he muttered against her skin.

"Mmm," was all she could manage.

"And this?" His hand left her breast to reach down between her legs, touching her where a woman always likes to be touched.

"Yes," she choked out, squirming with pleasure. "No. Yes. No, don't. Stop it. I'll come."

"But I love it when you come. Come for me, Celia. Don't try to stop it. Let yourself go. A-h-h, yes. *Yes!*"

Once again, they climaxed together, and the pleasure was blinding. But, far too soon, it was over and reality came back to scorn her.

See? You're addicted to him already. You can't say no. He only has to touch you and you melt.

Self-disgust had her forcibly moving away from him whilst her recent release gave her some measure of will-power.

"Hey," he protested at his abrupt ejection from her

body, but she didn't answer him. She scrambled off the bed and bolted for the bathroom, locking the door behind her.

Luke sighed and fell back on the bed. He knew exactly what was bothering Celia. The same thing that had bothered him when he'd first woken up.

Guilt.

He'd tried to ignore his conscience, had tried to forget that he was still engaged to Isabel. And he'd managed, for the few minutes he'd been making love to Celia just now. Hard to think of anything much when he was inside that hot little body of hers.

But the reality of his fiancée had still been waiting there, at the back of his mind.

Now, it was well to the foreground, a problem he could no longer push aside.

Isabel deserved better than this kind of behaviour from him. Celia deserved better, too.

He wasn't being fair to either of them.

But what was he to do for the best?

Okay, so he didn't love Isabel. But he didn't believe he loved Celia, either. As he'd told her, love didn't happen that quickly. It wasn't love that had first driven him into Celia's bed yesterday. It had been a wicked combination of things: her beauty and sensuality; her tears and his own grief over his parents' deaths. His recent celibacy hadn't helped either.

But perhaps the most insidiously corrupting factor in all this had been his initial misconception over Celia's role in his father's life. His male mind had been set onto a seductively sexual path from the moment he'd clapped eyes on her, a dark decadent path that had somehow perversely appealed to his present frustrated state of mind and body.

His threat to take her to hell with him last night might have been borne out of that, but he hadn't taken her to hell, had he? She'd taken him to heaven, as she'd promised.

What a surprising lover she'd turned out to be!

So enchantingly sweet in the beginning. But in the end, so amazingly bold.

Luke heard the shower being snapped on and his mind shot back to last night, to the two occasions they'd showered together. How startled she'd been the first time when he'd taken the shower gel and had washed her with it. All over. Her eyes had grown wider by the second. Clearly, her sexual experience was very limited.

On their second visit, however, it had been her to take the vanilla-scented gel in her hands, pouring it into her palm and massaging him with it in all sorts of equally intimate places. One in particular. His gut twisted just thinking about how incredible *that* had felt.

Her newly discovered wantonness had excited him. Unbearably. He'd especially loved it when she'd gone down him later. Because he'd known she hadn't done that before, either. She hadn't done anything much before, from what he could gather.

Not like Isabel.

He grimaced. Isabel, again.

He'd honestly thought he was happy with Isabel in bed. And he was. Or he had been.

But it was never going to be the same again, was it? He'd never be able to go to bed with her in the future without thinking of Celia, without wanting her to *be* Celia.

Regardless of what his feelings were for Celia, and vice versa, she'd ruined the idea of his marrying Isabel. Because he knew he would not be able to stay away from her. Not for long. There was nothing for it but to call the wedding off. And the sooner the better. Today, in fact.

Luke threw back the sheet and swung his feet over the side of the bed, scowling as he glanced around the room. His clothes... Where were his clothes?

Downstairs, he remembered, all over the place.

Sighing, he rose and padded down the stairs where he collected his discarded clothes and dragged them all back on, minus the tie which he shoved into his jacket pocket. Then he picked up Celia's things, shaking his head over her ripped panties. He'd been like an animal!

But she'd seemed to like it. She seemed to like anything he did to her. She was going to be very pleased when he told her he was calling the wedding off.

Isabel wasn't, though. She was going to be upset. So were her parents. Nice people, both of them. Not wealthy, either. He hated the thought of doing this to all three of them.

At least he was rich enough now to make financial recompense for any expenses they couldn't recoup. He'd give Isabel a packet, too. She deserved it.

But no amount of money, he knew, would make up for the distress he was going to cause.

Celia opened the bathroom door just as Luke made it to the top of the stairs with her clothes. She had a towel wrapped around her head and was wearing a satiny cream robe. But not another darn thing, by the way the silky material clung to her skin as she walked into the room. It was going to be difficult doing the right thing and keeping his resolve to leave.

Only the thought of his imminent return—could he get back by tonight?—kept him focused.

Her eyes showed shock when she first noted his dressed state. But they swiftly grew cold and almost contemptuous. "You're leaving, I see," she bit out.

"Yes, I am," he began. "But I—"

"Please don't say another word," she snapped. "It's not necessary. I'm quite glad you're leaving. Now I don't have to ask you to, and there won't be a scene."

He frowned at her, wondering exactly what was behind this sudden change of attitude. After all, this was the girl who'd promised to keep him in heaven all weekend, who'd declared her undying love.

"Are you still angry with me about Isabel, is that it?" he asked, placing her clothes on the foot of the bed.

"No, that's not it." She reefed the towel off her head and her hair tumbled around her shoulders, a mass of damp dark red curls. She started rubbing it dry, and not quite looking at him. "The thing is, Luke, I realised this morning that you were right and I was wrong. I don't love you. It's just a sexual thing between us."

He frowned at her. How odd, he thought, that listening to her say what he'd actually said to her would make him see *he'd* been the one who was wrong. It wasn't just sex between them. It was something far stronger and far more special.

"Look, I won't be a hypocrite and say I didn't enjoy myself last night," she said, sweeping on. "I did. It was a real eye-opener. And an education all right. You've taught me how to come on cue and how to please a man, and for that I'm grateful. But given you *are* engaged, I'd rather leave things at a one-night stand. So thank you, but goodbye."

Luke could not believe what he was hearing. In fact, he *didn't* believe it. "You're lying to me," he stated firmly.

Her eyes finally met his. Such beautiful, expressive eyes when she wasn't acting. Clear windows to her soul, her frightened, hurt, sensitive soul.

"Why on earth would I do that?" she threw at him.

If she thought she could hide her vulnerability behind some falsely assertive façade, then she was way wrong. "Pride?" he suggested softly. "Conscience? Fear?"

"Fear?"

"Yes. You're worried that we'll end up like your mother and my father."

That rattled her. "And if I am, don't you think I have a right to be? I'd be a fool to think you're going to call off your marriage to Isabel because of me."

"But I am," he said.

She stared at him for a few startled moments, then laughed. "Oh, please. Don't insult my intelligence. Why would you do that? You've already said you don't love me, that you'd never give up the substance for the shadow. You're the one who's lying, and we both know why. You don't want to give up the great sex we had last night just yet.''

"No. I don't want to give *you* up, Celia. There's a difference.''

"No.'' She began shaking her head violently. "No, I can't afford to believe that kind of thing.''

"Then, I guess it's up to me to *make* you believe me. I will be back, Celia. Today.''

"Well, I won't be here.'' Again, she flashed defiant eyes at him, and he almost smiled. A man who didn't know her as well as he did might have been fooled. But he *did* know her well, much better than he knew Isabel.

Strange, that.

"Yes, you will,'' he said. "You'll wait for me.''

"And what makes you so sure of that?''

"Because you have to. Just as I have to come back. We were meant to be together, Celia. It was our destiny.''

"Our destiny?''

"Yes. You were the one who was right and I was wrong. We *have* fallen in love. I tried to argue against it in my mind but I can see that was very foolish of me. Because you can't argue with emotion. I've fallen in love with you, Celia. And you've fallen in love with me. End of story. Or should I say, the beginning of our story, if you want it to be. It's up to you.''

Celia stared at him. She wanted to believe him more than anything else in the world. But it was so hard to rise above everything she'd come to believe about men.

Yet, to be fair, Luke wasn't just an ordinary man. He

was an exceptional man. Sensitive. Kind. Deep. If she didn't trust *him*, then she'd never trust any man. Which meant she'd never have the things her mother never had, and which she'd always craved: a partner for life who loved her and wanted to have children with her.

She looked at Luke and wanted to have a family with him so very much. He'd be a wonderful father, she knew.

She had to believe in him. Because not to would make her such a coward. And she wasn't that.

"Yes. I…I'll be here," she admitted shakily, knowing that if he betrayed that trust, if he didn't return today, she would never recover.

"And I'll be back," he promised, coming forward to give her a polite peck on the cheek.

When his head lifted she gazed longingly up into his eyes. "Kiss me properly."

"I don't dare. You have great power in your lips, my love."

Her heart tightened. "Am I, Luke?" she whispered, her voice catching. "Am I really your love?"

He groaned, then swept her into his arms, his lips crushing down on hers.

She clung to him when his mouth finally lifted.

"Don't go," she said, sobbing.

"I don't want to. I *have* to. You yourself said you can't find happiness over the misery of others. I can't in all conscience leave it any longer to tell Isabel I'm not going to marry her. I promise I'll be back by dark. If I'm delayed for any reason, I'll ring. Come downstairs and write down your mobile number for me."

Celia knew he was right to go. But still, she didn't want him to.

"Hurry back," she called after him as he drove off. He waved, and was gone.

CHAPTER TWELVE

ISABEL'S parents lived in a neat federation-style home in the inner Sydney suburb of Burwood. An elderly couple, they'd given Luke the impression that they'd been very relieved when their youngest child had finally found a man she wanted to marry.

Isabel didn't look like a rebel, but Luke suspected she'd given her parents a few worries over the years. She'd had lots of jobs. Lots of lovers too, he'd gathered, though he was pretty sure her parents didn't know that.

Isabel was not a girl who confided often, or in great detail. They'd never had deep and meaningful discussions about their past relationships, just their future together. All Luke knew about Isabel's previous lovers were that they were losers, and she no longer trusted herself to fall in love with anyone fit for marriage and fatherhood. Which was why she'd decided to marry with her head, rather than her heart.

Luke wasn't quite sure what Isabel's reaction would be to his breaking off their engagement. No doubt she'd be upset and disappointed, but he doubted she'd be destroyed. No, definitely not destroyed.

Her parents would probably be *more* upset.

As Luke approached their house shortly before one, he was relieved to think that they would have already left for their regular Saturday afternoon's bowling down at their local club. Much better to tell Isabel by herself first.

Luke had rung her parents' number on the drive down, because that was where Isabel was staying till the wedding, but she hadn't been home. Apparently, she'd received a call that morning from the photographer she'd booked for the wedding with the news he'd broken a leg in a water-skiing accident and would not be able to do their wedding after all.

When he'd first heard this news, Luke had thought *good*. That was one thing they wouldn't have to cancel. But unfortunately, their accident-prone photographer had recommended a colleague and Isabel had already gone to meet this new chap.

"She just rang a little while back and she said she'd be home by one at the latest," her mother had trilled down the line.

Luke had thought about ringing Isabel on her mobile at the time but decided against it. He couldn't trust his voice not to betray something, and he wanted to deliver his news face to face.

Luke regretted that decision now as he slid his car into the kerb outside Isabel's front gate, because there was no sign of her stylish little navy car anywhere around.

It wasn't like Isabel at all to be late for anything and he wondered if fate was conspiring against him today. In desperation, he rang her mobile phone but she didn't answer. Another unusual occurrence, leaving him no option but to sit there and wait. Twenty agitating minutes passed before he spied her car in the side mirror coming round the corner from the main road.

His stomach was buzzing with butterflies by the time she parked behind him. How he hated having to do this.

They both climbed out from behind their wheels simultaneously, Isabel throwing him a startled look. "Luke! What on earth are you doing here? I wasn't expecting you. Why didn't you call me?"

She looked beautiful as usual, but not quite her usual, serene self. Her hair was slightly mussed and she looked flushed in the cheeks as well. He supposed the photographer business had upset her.

His timing couldn't have been worse.

"I tried your mobile a little while back," he said. "But you didn't answer."

"What? Oh, I must have left the blasted thing behind at the studio. I took it out to ring Mum and tell her how long I'd be. Oh, too bad," she muttered, slamming the car door. "It can stay there till tomorrow. I'm not going back now."

She shook her head and threw Luke a pained look. "You've no idea the dreadful day I've had. The photographer I booked for the wedding's had an accident and he made an appointment for me to meet with this other man who's not really suitable at all. Brilliant, but one of those avant-garde types who wants to do everything in black and white. I pointed out that I wouldn't have selected a wine-red gown for my maid of honour to wear if I'd wanted all the shots done in black and white. I was being sarcastic, of course, but would he listen to me? No! He even told me how he wanted me to wear my hair. As if I don't know what suits me best. I've never met such an insufferably opinionated man.''

Wow! Luke had never known Isabel to rave on like this. And she hadn't finished yet!

''Still, what can you expect from someone who fancies himself an artiste. You know the type. Struts around like he's God's gift to women. And he wears this earring in the shape of a phantom's head, of all things. What a show pony! Lord knows what our photographs are going to turn out like, but it's simply too late to get someone else decent,'' she muttered, before lifting a frustrated face.

''His name's Rafe, did I tell you? Rafe Saint Vincent. It wouldn't be his real name, of course. Just a career move. Nobody is born with a name like Rafe Saint Vincent. Talk about pretentious!''

Luke wished Isabel's tirade would come to a halt. He was feeling worse and worse by the moment. Carrying on like this was so unlike Isabel. This Rafe chap had really gotten under her skin. And now here he was, about to drop an even bigger bombshell.

Maybe she finally got the vibes, because she suddenly stopped ranting and stared at him. ''You know, Luke, you look like you've slept in your clothes. And you haven't even shaved. That's not like you at all. What are you doing here, anyway? I thought you were going to stay in your father's old fishing cabin up on Lake Macquarie for the whole weekend.''

"The cabin wasn't there any more. It had been torn down a few years before."

"Oh, what a shame. So where did you stay last night? In a motel? Or a tent?" she added drily, looking him up and down.

"No, Dad had built a brand new weekender on the same site. I stayed there."

"But—" she broke off and frowned "—how did you get in? You didn't break in, did you?"

"No, there was a girl staying there for the weekend and she let me in."

Isabel looked taken aback. "And she let you *sleep* the night?"

Luke sighed. "It's a long story, Isabel. I think we'd better go inside and sit down while I tell it to you."

She threw him an alarmed look. "Luke, you're worrying me..."

He took her arm and started propelling her over to the gate, but she pulled out of his grip and lanced him with panicky eyes. "You're not going ahead with the wedding, are you?"

He pressed his lips tightly together. No point in lying to her. "No," he confessed. "No, I'm not."

Luke was stunned when his oh, so pragmatic fiancée took this news very badly indeed.

"Oh, no," she cried. "No, Luke, don't do this to me!" And she buried her stricken face in her hands.

For the third time in the last twenty-four hours, Luke took a weeping woman into his arms and tried to comfort her.

"I'm so sorry, Isabel," he said.

"But why?" she cried quite angrily against his shirt, her hands gripping the lapels of his jacket and shaking them. *"Why?"*

"I've fallen in love."

Her eyes jerked up, shocked and sceptical. "Fallen in love! In less than a day?"

"No one is more surprised than me, I can tell you. But it's true. I came back straight away to tell you, and to call our wedding off."

"But love's no guarantee of happiness, Luke. I thought we agreed on that. It traps you and tricks you. It really is blind. This girl you've supposedly fallen in love with so quickly," she said, scornfully, "how do you know she'll be good for you? How do you know she won't make you miserable? You can't possibly know her real character, not this quickly. She could be playing a part for you, pretending to be something she's not. She might be a really bad person. A gold-digger, perhaps. A…a criminal, even!"

Luke was shocked by the extreme vehemence in Isabel's speculations. Clearly, someone at some time had hurt Isabel very badly. Some pretender. And whilst that thought made him understand her better, he was no longer able to embrace her once-bitten, forever careful cynicism.

True, he'd once thought he didn't want love and passion. But, since hearing his mother's history, Luke had worked out that strong emotions sometimes dredged up bad tapes from his early childhood, like when his mother had been unstable. Luke still didn't relish angry confrontations nor shouting matches, but he could no longer turn his back on the power and pleasure of true love. He felt confident that once his personal problems had been ironed out, his relationship with Celia would also bring the peace and contentment he was looking for. Because Celia, too, wanted that, he was sure.

"She's not any of those things," he told Isabel. "She's a good person. I just know it."

Isabel just shook her head. "I would never have believed you could be so naïve. A man like you!"

"I'm not naïve. Which is why I'm not rushing into anything. But I can't marry *you*, Isabel, feeling as I do about Celia. Surely you can see that."

Isabel let his lapels go with a disgruntled sigh. "Maybe I do and maybe I don't. *I'd* still marry *you*. I haven't much time for the highly overrated state of being *in love*."

"Maybe that's because you've never really been in love," Luke pointed out, and Isabel laughed.

"I'm an expert on the subject. But that's all right. You'll live and learn, Luke Freeman and, when you do, give me a call. Meanwhile, let's go inside as you said. I think I need a drink. Not tea or coffee. Something much stronger. Dad still has some of the whisky I gave him for his birthday. That should do the trick."

Luke frowned as he followed her into her parents' house. "But you don't drink Scotch?"

"Ah but I do," she threw over her shoulder at him as she strode into the lounge and over to the small drinks cabinet which held a small selection of decanters and glasses. "When the occasion calls for it," she added, and poured herself half a glassful. "Which is now. Today. This very second." And she quaffed back a darned good swallow. "Ah," she said with a lip-smacking sigh. "That hits the spot."

Luke couldn't help staring at her. This wasn't the Isabel he knew. This was someone else. She even *talked* differently.

"You want one?" she asked, and he shook his head.

Rolling the rest of the amber liquid in the glass, she walked over and curled herself up in one of the deep armchairs, her feet tucked under her. Scooping her blonde hair back from her face with one hand and lifting the glass to her lips with her other, she looked like some *femme fatale* from a *film noire*. If Luke hadn't been crazy about Celia he might have regretted breaking his engagement to this suddenly intriguing chameleon of a woman. If nothing else, life with her might have held more surprises than he'd been anticipating.

"I suppose she's beautiful, this Celia," Isabel said in dry tones.

"I think so." Luke settled himself in the chair opposite. No point in staying standing.

"What does she do?"

"She's a physiotherapist."

"And what was she doing, staying in your father's weekender? Did he rent it out, did he?"

"No. She was his mistress's daughter," he stated

rather baldly. But he was determined to tell Isabel the whole truth. She deserved nothing less.

"His *what*?" Isabel's feet shot out from under her as she snapped forward on the chair. Her glass, which was already approaching empty, remained frozen in mid-air.

"Dad's mistress's daughter," Luke repeated ruefully.

"No! I don't believe you. Not *your* Dad. With a *mistress*? That's impossible! He was one of the best husbands and fathers I've ever met. He was one of the reasons I wanted to marry *you*. Because I believed you'd be just as good a family man."

"As I said," Luke said drily, "it's a long story."

"And a fascinating one, I'm sure. It seems the Freeman men have a dark side I don't know about."

"Could be."

"I wish I'd known about it sooner," she muttered, and swigged back another mind-numbing mouthful of Scotch.

"What do you mean by that?"

"Oh, nothing. Just a private joke. I have this perverse sense of humour sometimes. Come on, tell me all the naughty details."

"I hope you won't be too shocked."

She chuckled. "Oh, dear, that's funny. Me, shocked? Trust me, darling. I can never be seriously shocked by anything sexual."

Luke looked at her with thoughtful eyes. "Did I ever really know you, Isabel?"

"Did I ever really know *you*?" she countered saucily.

Their eyes met and they both smiled together.

"You'll find someone else, Isabel," Luke said with total confidence.

"I dare say I will," she agreed. "But not quite like you, darling. You were one in a million. Your Celia is one lucky girl. I hope you'll be very happy together."

"Thanks, Isabel. That's very generous of you. But we won't be rushing to the altar. Which reminds me…I will, of course, be footing the bill for any expenses your parents have encountered with the wedding. I'll send them a cheque which should cover everything, and with some left over. And I'll be doing the right thing by you, too."

She shook her head as she slipped her solitaire-diamond engagement ring off her finger. "No, Luke. I wasn't marrying you for your money. I know you might have thought I was, but I wasn't. I was just pleased you were successful and stable. I wanted that security for my children. And for myself."

"I don't want that ring back, Isabel. It's yours. I gave it to you. You keep it, or sell it, if you want to."

She shrugged and slipped it onto a finger on her right hand. "If you insist. But I won't sell it. I'll wear it. It's a beautiful ring. Fortunate, though, that I didn't find any wedding rings I liked yesterday, so at least we won't have to return them. I'd better go get you your credit card while you're here."

"That can wait," he said before she could get up. "I want to finish discussing the rest of my financial obligations first."

She frowned. "What other financial obligations could you possibly have?"

"I owe you, Isabel. More than a ring's worth."

"No, you don't, Luke. I never lived with you. I have no claim on you, other than the expenses for the wedding."

"That's not the way I see it. You gave up your job to become my wife. You expected to be going on your honeymoon in a fortnight's time and possibly becoming a mother in the near future. Aside from that, married to me, you would never have had to worry about money for the rest of your life. I can't help you with the honeymoon or the becoming-a-mother bit now, but I can give you the financial security for life that you deserved."

"Luke, truly, you don't have to do this."

"Yes. I do. Now listen up. Firstly, I want you to have my town house in Turramurra. I'm temporarily moving back into the family home to live, so I don't need it. The furniture, too. It wouldn't fit any other place, anyway. You already have a key, don't you?"

"Yes, but…"

"No more buts, Isabel, please. The place is yours. I'll also have Harvey set up an investment portfolio for you as well which will give you a regular income for life. Only blue-chip stocks and shares. Nothing risky."

Isabel looked shocked. "But Luke, can you afford to do all that?"

"My father was a very rich man, and now so am I."

"I see. But still—"

"Call it conscience money, if you like, but please don't say no."

She thought about it for a few moments, then shrugged. "All right, Luke. I won't. I'd be a fool to, wouldn't I?"

"Absolutely."

She smiled a wry smile at him. "I always knew you were a winner. But I'd have preferred you as my husband, rather than my sugar daddy."

Luke sighed. "You've no idea how sorry I am about all this, Isabel. I wouldn't have hurt you for the world. You're a great girl. But the moment I saw Celia, I was a goner."

"She must be something, this Celia."

"She's very special."

"Okay, so tell me all. And don't leave out anything just because you think it might shock me. I told you. I can't be shocked in matters of the flesh. I'm not in love with you, so I won't be eaten up with jealousy."

Isabel was wrong. She *was* shocked. Goggle-eyed, to put it mildly, mostly by the length of his father's affair with Celia's mother.

"I still can't believe it of Lionel. He just didn't seem to be the type. Do you think he was really in love with Celia's mother all along, or was it just a sexual arrangement because of your mum's...er...personal problems?" she finished delicately.

"I honestly don't know. I'd like to think he loved her..."

"But you aren't sure that he did. And you'll never

know now, will you? And neither will that poor woman.
I feel terribly sorry for her. She must feel like her whole
life's been wasted.''

Luke shook his head. ''I have to confess I'm still very
disappointed with Dad. Yet, who am I to judge, Isabel?
This last twenty-four hours has taught me that we're all
just human beings, with flaws and failings by the
dozen.''

''You can say that again. We also always think we'd
do things differently if we had our lives over again,''
Isabel mused, ''but we probably wouldn't. We'd probably make the same stupid mistakes all over again. And
again. And again.''

Luke cocked his head on one side and looked at her.
''So what mistakes are you referring to? Would I be far
out if I thought it had something to do with your falling
in love with the wrong type of man in the past?''

She laughed. ''I think it's too late for that kind of
confidence, darling heart. Besides, I want to leave you
thinking of me as the very sensible creature you liked
and admired enough to consider marrying.''

''And you're not so sensible?''

''I was with you.''

''But not with other men?''

''Not with a couple of them. And one in particular.''

''I see...''

She laughed again. ''No, you don't. And you never
will. Now, I'll go get you that credit card of yours...''

She was gone before he could say Jack Robinson,
leaving him to speculate on the type of woman she'd

been with other men. But she was back before his male mind went too far down that road.

"I presume you'll be returning to your Celia now?" she asked as she walked with him out to his car.

"I have to drop in at home first and pick up some clothes. But, yes, I'll be driving back up there as soon as I can."

"Drive carefully. And Luke..."

"Yes?"

"Thank you for the town house and the money. I do appreciate it. You really didn't have to, you know."

"I know. It was my pleasure. I'll get Harvey onto the paperwork first thing Monday morning."

"Whenever."

"No, the sooner the better. I'll also write a big fat cheque for your parents when I get back home, and pop it straight in a mailbox this very afternoon. What about the various cancellations for the wedding? Do you need any help with those?"

"No, I'll handle them. I'm the only one who knows everything, anyway. Mum left most of the arrangements up to me. She knows how stubborn I can be when I want something a certain way."

Luke blinked his surprise. Didn't sound like the very accommodating Isabel *he* knew.

But then, he didn't know her, did he? Not down deep.

"Thank heavens people haven't started sending gifts yet," she went on, bringing his mind back to practicalities.

"What about the honeymoon? You won't get anything back for that, even if you do ring and cancel. It's all prepaid and too late to expect any refund. Why don't we send your parents in our place?''

Isabel smiled. ''You're just trying to suck up to them so that they don't kill you.''

Luke grinned. ''Absolutely.''

''That's not such a bad idea. Mum was quite jealous when she found out where we were going. She said she'd always wanted to have a holiday on one of the Barrier Reef islands.''

''Good. I'll pop the plane tickets and the details in the envelope with the cheque.''

''You're being very generous, Luke.''

''I feel very guilty.''

''And so you should,'' she said, but with a smile.

''At least you won't need to hire that irritating photographer now,'' he pointed out.

Her left eyebrow arched in a sardonic fashion. ''You're right,'' she said wryly. ''That's certainly a bonus.''

''But you still have to go back and get your phone,'' Luke reminded her.

''I suppose I shall,'' she said. ''Now…''

''I must fly, Isabel. I promised Celia I'd be back by dark.''

''Off you go, then. And do take care.''

''I will.''

Luke drove off with a much lighter heart than he'd arrived with. Isabel had given him a fright there for a moment, crying like that. But things had worked out reasonably well in the end.

Hopefully, she would fall in love one day. And not with some loser this time. Meanwhile, he'd make sure she didn't lack anything, financially.

Now, all Luke wanted to do was get back to Celia.

As soon as he arrived home, he went upstairs and showered and shaved, got dressed in casual clothes, packed a few more things in a bag, collected the honeymoon plane tickets from where he'd put them a few days before then hurried downstairs to his father's study.

It was a large room, large and masculine, with dark wooden furniture, book-lined walls and everything a successful man could wish for.

Luke sat down at the desk and ran his hands back and forth across the large leather top. It had never been this tidy when his father had been alive. It had always been littered with papers and plans and the monthly magazines his dad subscribed to. Ones about computers and fishing and wine. They had been his hobbies.

Aside from his mistress, of course, came the suddenly depressing thought.

Luke sighed then opened the drawers which he knew contained the things he wanted. Blank cheques. Stationery. Stamps. He'd gone through the desk the week before, a lousy job, worse even than going through his parents' wardrobes. There, he'd just given everything away to charity. His father's personal papers, however, had required more careful and personal attention and there were some things he simply hadn't been able to throw away. Not yet, anyway.

Ten minutes later the cheque for Isabel's parents was written and slipped into a business-sized envelope, along with a small letter of sincere apology and the plane tickets. Luke stuck on a stamp, addressed and sealed the envelope. All he had to do after that was pop it into a postbox somewhere.

Luke slid back the swivel chair from the desk and was about to stand up when his eyes dropped down under the desk and a memory struck from his childhood. He'd been playing in here one day without permission, pretending to be a cat burglar, if he recalled rightly. He'd been all of eight at the time and had just seen a movie about cat burglars on the television.

When he'd heard someone at the door, he'd dashed under the desk and had hidden there. A stupid place, if it had been his father coming in. But he'd been lucky. It had been his mother. She'd only stayed a minute or two and she hadn't seen him hiding under the desk. But, during that time, Luke had noticed a button built into the underrim of the desk. When his mother had left the room, he'd pressed it, and a secret drawer had shot out.

It had been disappointingly empty that time, and every subsequent time he'd snuck in to look in it. After a year or so, Luke had lost interest and had forgotten all about it.

But having thought of it now, he fished under the desk with his fingers and pressed the secret button. The drawer slid out, but it wasn't empty this time. It contained a couple of sheets of writing paper, folded over.

Luke picked them up and unfolded them, his heart racing with anticipation. The writing was definitely his father's and it was a letter, which began, "My Dearest Jess..."

Luke hesitated. It had been drummed into him from childhood never to read another person's mail. But this hadn't even been posted and he just had to read it, had to hopefully find out what kind of man his father had really been.

The letter was quite long. Two full pages.

Luke took ages reading, then rereading them.

By the time his head lifted, tears had filled his eyes.

He just sat there for ages, blinking, thinking.

"Yes," he muttered at last. "Dad's right. That's what he should have done and that's what I should do."

Rising, he popped the letter in his bag, picked up the other envelope and bag, and left the house, locking up after him. He threw his bag into the boot then climbed in behind the wheel, placing the envelope addressed to Isabel's parents on the passenger seat, intending to pop it into the first postbox he saw.

But as soon as he started heading north, Luke forgot all about that envelope, his head full of other things. Distracting things.

He'd been on the motorway for ages before he remembered.

He groaned, annoyed with himself.

Suddenly, he saw the sign saying the turn-off for

Gosford was coming up. There was sure to be a postbox there. Luke slowed then decided it would be silly to detour when the mail didn't even go at the weekends. He could easily post it on the Monday.

Having decided to keep on going, Luke sped up again. Unfortunately, the car travelling alongside him chose that same moment to accelerate and cut in ahead of him to take the exit.

Luke pulled his wheel to the left, breaking at the same time, but it was too late. They collided, metal crunching, brakes screeching, tyres smoking, both cars hurtling towards the side of the road.

Luke didn't even have time to swear before they hit the rock faces awaiting them and everything went black.

CHAPTER THIRTEEN

CELIA paced the deck, every now and then hurrying down the steps and going round the side of the house to stand and peer through the trees, hoping to see Luke's blue BMW coming along the road.

But it was never there. And now, it was nearly dark.

He'd promised to be back by dark.

Darkness fell and still, no sign of Luke. And no phone call, explaining why he'd been delayed. She wished she'd thought to ask him for *his* mobile number, but she hadn't. She did find Lionel's home number via directory enquiries. But there was no answer.

Eight o'clock came. Then nine. Then ten. Celia couldn't eat. Nor watch TV. She just paced the living room instead of the deck, every now and then going to the back door, opening it and peering into the night, looking for car lights.

By midnight Celia was forced to accept Luke wasn't going to come back. Not that night. Not ever.

It was at that moment she realised just how much she loved the man. Because the thought of never seeing him again was so overwhelming, she wasn't sure she could live with it. She couldn't breathe, couldn't think. All she knew was that she had to see him again, had to be with him again, no matter what.

"Marry Isabel, if that's what you want," she wailed to the empty room, "but don't leave me like this. Just let me see you every now and then. Let me…"

She broke off, appalled by what she'd just said, and what she was prepared to do to see Luke again. She *was* no better than her mother, whom she'd condemned all these years for being weak-willed and wishy-washy. If she couldn't learn from her mother's mistakes then what kind of fool was she?

A fool finally, deeply, insanely in love.

Celia began to cry then. She cried and cried and cried till she could cry no more. Finally, she fell asleep on the sofa, still clinging to the faint hope that Luke might turn up, that some circumstance of fate had prevented him from returning.

She awoke to daylight and someone gently shaking her shoulder, her heart leaping even in her half-asleep state.

"Luke?" she said before her brain registered it was her mother who'd roused her.

"*Luke?*" her mother repeated, frowning down at her daughter. "Why would you think I would be Luke?"

"What?" Celia pretended to be a bit fuzzy from sleep. "Sorry. I've just woken up. I'm still half asleep."

Her mother gave her a narrow-eyed look, her eyes taking in her daughter's appearance in one glance.

Celia knew she must look a mess after all the crying she'd done, plus sleeping in her clothes.

"So what are *you* doing here, Mum?" she countered swiftly as distraction.

It worked, her mother looking quite happily around the room now, rather than at her.

"I just couldn't wait to see the place again, now that this lovely house is going to be all mine. I didn't come yesterday because of what you said about needing some peace and quiet this weekend, but I thought you wouldn't mind my spending a few hours here today."

"You drove yourself, did you?"

"No. Helen wouldn't let me. She said I wasn't ready to drive yet, which is silly. I feel perfectly fine now. So much better after Luke's visit. But you know your aunt. Such a worrywart."

Celia thought that was a bit unfair. And just a tad ungrateful. Aunt Helen had been marvellous.

"Aunt Helen dropped you off, did she?" Celia asked as she swung her legs over the side of the sofa.

"Yes. She couldn't come in. She has to get ready to go to some luncheon with John at their club today. She saw your car was still here and asked if you could possibly drop me back at her place late this afternoon."

"Oh. Okay." The prospect of having her mother here all day was an awkward one. She hated the thought of having to hide her misery and act normal, when all she wanted to do was cry some more.

"I know it's out of your way," Jessica said, perhaps picking up on her daughter's reluctance.

"It's no trouble, Mum. Truly."

Jessica sighed. "Yes, it is. I've been nothing but trouble since Lionel died and I feel quite guilty about it. Trust me, come tomorrow I'm not going to be a burden any longer. I'm going to get my car back and I'm going to move back in here. I know it's not officially my place as yet, but I'm sure Luke wouldn't mind. Such a kind, generous man.''

The appalling thought crossed Celia's mind that maybe this house would never be her mother's now. Maybe Luke had changed his mind over lots of things, not just returning to her. Maybe he wanted nothing more to do with any of the Gilbert women and was going to marry Isabel in a fortnight's time, as planned.

Such thinking brought the deepest, darkest despair.

But, he couldn't marry her. *Could* he?

''What is it, Celia?'' her mother asked worriedly. ''What's wrong?''

''Nothing, I—I—''

''Please don't try to fob me off. I know there's something wrong. You think I haven't noticed you've been crying? On top of that, why did you sleep down here on the sofa when there's a perfectly good bed upstairs?''

Her mother sank down beside her on the sofa and placed a loving arm around her shoulders. Celia tensed, holding onto the last of her emotional control like some mountain climber gripping a cliff, knowing that to let go would be the end.

''There *is* something wrong, isn't there?'' her mother probed gently. ''Something to do with Luke Freeman, if I'm any guess. You didn't call out his name for nothing. And just then, when I brought his name up again, you looked very unhappy. You like him a lot, don't you? And you're upset because he's going to marry someone else.''

''Oh, Mum!'' Celia cried, and burst into tears.

''Oh, Celia…'' Her mother smoothed her hair gently back from her face as she used to when she'd been a child. ''I'm so sorry, darling. So sorry. I—'' She pulled back suddenly. ''What's this?'' And her fingers went to touch the love bite on her neck.

Celia's hand flew up to try and hide it, but her mother grabbed her hand and stared with uncompromising eyes into her own.

''If you think I don't know what that is, then you can think again, daughter of mine. Did Luke give that to you?''

Celia blushed.

''The bastard!'' Jessica spat. ''The miserable bastard. When? On Friday night after he left Helen's, when he was supposed to be driving home to his fiancée?''

Celia shook her head. ''No. Earlier.''

''*Earlier!* But you only met him that afternoon! Celia, how could you?''

''Oh, Mum, don't come that holier-than-thou stuff with me. You, of all people, should appreciate what happened. It was like it was with you and Lionel. The moment he took me in his arms, I couldn't even think straight.''

''And why, pray tell, did he take you in his arms in the first place?'' Jessica asked with barely held anger.

''Because I was crying.''

''Crying! Why were you crying?''

"What does that matter now? I was upset, about you and Lionel. And he was upset, about you and Lionel. We comforted each other and then we went to bed and it…it was fantastic! You must remember what that was like, don't you?" she threw at her mother in frustration and exasperation. "That's why *you* kept letting Lionel back into your bed, isn't it? Because you couldn't live without the way you felt when he was there. Well, I can't live without the way I feel when I'm with Luke. The trouble is I stupidly thought he couldn't live without the way he felt when he was with me. He said he'd break his engagement to Isabel and come back to me. But he hasn't," she cried, tears streaming down her face. "He's gone and changed his mind, that's what he's done. And I don't want to live any more," she wailed. "Do you know how that feels, Mum?"

Celia's words hung in the air. Charged and challenging.

"Yes," Jessica bit out. "I know exactly how that feels. And to think I thought Luke was so nice. A real gentleman. *Men!*" she sneered. "They're all the same. Especially the handsome ones. They think they can get away with anything. The trouble is," she added angrily, "usually, they can."

"I thought he loved me," Celia said, sobbing, and threw herself into her mother's arms again.

"I know, darling, I know. I thought Lionel loved me too. But he didn't. Not the way I loved him. If he had, he would have left his wife for me, just as your Luke would have left his Isabel. But he didn't, did he? He went back to her like they always do.''

The doorbell ringing had both women's heads snapping round to stare at the door, then at each other.

''Do you think…?'' Celia began, her heart pounding with instant hope.

''I don't know. Let's go and see.''

Celia raced to the door and wrenched it open. A policeman stood there, looking grave.

Celia's heart began plummeting down into a place it had never been before, a yawning black pit which went on and on and on.

Luke. Something had happened to Luke.

''Miss Gilbert?'' he said. ''Miss Jessica Gilbert?''

Celia almost fainted with relief. It wasn't her he wanted. He hadn't come to tell her Luke was dead.

''I'm Jessica Gilbert,'' her mother intervened, taking Celia firmly by the shoulders and holding her upright. ''This is my daughter, Celia. What's the problem, officer?''

''Gosford Hospital has been trying to contact you, ma'am, but didn't know your phone number or your address. They asked us for help and we were able to come up with this address from details on your driver's licence.'' The policeman pulled out a small notebook and consulted it before continuing. ''It seems a gentleman friend of your daughter, a Mr Luke Freeman, was in a car accident on the motorway late yesterday afternoon.''

Celia made some sort of whimpering sound and the policeman looked at her with kind eyes.

"He's alive, miss. But he is in intensive care and still unconscious."

Relief and worry mingled to overwhelm Celia. Oh, Luke, Luke, you *were* coming back to me, weren't you? I should never have doubted you.

She lifted teary eyes to her mother. "I have to go, Mum. Straight away."

"I'll drive you," Jessica offered. "You're not in a fit state."

"But..."

"Let your mother do the driving, miss," the policeman insisted.

Celia didn't like to enlighten him that, lately, it had been her mother who hadn't been fit to drive. That was why Aunt Helen had confiscated her car. But it seemed her mother was well on the way to recovery if the determined look on her face was anything to go by. Family crises did bring out the best in a person. Celia had been there for her mother a couple of weeks back, and now her mother was here for her.

"Thanks, Mum," she said with a sniffle or two. "I'll just run to the bathroom, then get my purse."

"I'll be going, then," said the policeman.

Both women thanked him, and soon they were on their way to Gosford Hospital, a good forty-minute drive away. Neither woman spoke, with Celia wringing her hands whilst Jessica concentrated on the road. The turn-off for Gosford Hospital could not come quickly enough for Celia. Eventually, there it was, but they were still quite a few miles away.

"Direct me from here," her mother asked once they were back on the Pacific Highway which only had two lanes on that section and was quite windy and narrow. "You know these roads better than me. And Gosford Hospital, too."

Celia did, having worked there briefly the previous year.

She knew exactly where to park and how to find intensive care. Not the easiest part of the hospital to locate with a lift ride first, then long, seemingly endless, corridors and turnings. By the time they arrived at the ward sister's desk, Celia's nervous tension had increased a thousandfold with her stomach feeling as if it had been on the Wild Mouse Ride at Sydney's Luna Park.

The nurse behind the desk was a stranger to Celia, a tight-lipped, pudding-faced biddy with all the tact and charm of a taxation-department auditor.

"No, Mr Freeman isn't dead or dying," they were brusquely informed at which point Celia struggled not to burst into tears again. For they would have been wasted on this tartar. "He has a severe concussion, several broken ribs and extensive bruising down his right-hand side."

"Has he gained consciousness at all?" Celia asked anxiously.

"Mr Freeman came round briefly a while ago," the sister informed them. "But he had a shot of pethidine for the pain and is back asleep now."

"May we see him?"

The sister pursed her lips and frowned. "You're relatives, are you?"

"This is his girlfriend," Celia's mother piped up.

"*Another* girlfriend!"

"What do you mean, another girlfriend?"

"She means Isabel, Mum," Celia said with false calm. "Who else?"

"Yes, that's her name," the nurse confirmed. "Isabel."

Celia's heart sank once more. Maybe Luke hadn't been coming back to her at all. Maybe he'd just been coming to tell her he'd changed his mind and was going to marry Isabel.

"Celia?" a soft, female voice said from behind Celia's shoulder. "That *is* you, isn't it?"

Celia turned slowly, almost afraid of what she would see.

And she had every right to be.

Isabel *was* beautiful. Coolly, classically beautiful with thickly lashed blue eyes, an English-rose complexion and silky fair hair, which was sleekly up in a French roll with not a strand out of place. She was wearing a tailored cream linen trousers suit with a sky blue camisole underneath that matched the colour of her eyes.

Celia still had on the faded jeans and grey Sloppy Joe she'd dragged on late yesterday afternoon when the breeze off the lake had turned cool. She had not a scrap of make-up on and her hair was all over the place.

"I'm so glad the police were able to find you," Isabel said politely.

"I was at Mum's place," Celia replied, trying not to sound shaken by this woman's extraordinary beauty and composure. Impossible to call her a girl. She was a woman through and through. "She drove me down straight away."

"Naturally, Celia was too upset to drive," her mother pointed out a touch tartly.

"Naturally," Isabel agreed and, for the life of her, Celia could not detect any hint of sarcasm in the word.

So what was going on here?

There was only one way she was going to find out. Ask.

"Since you know about me," Celia said carefully, "then I presume Luke must have told you what—what happened this weekend?"

"Oh, yes. He was totally truthful. Explained how he'd fallen in love with you and that he couldn't possibly marry me, under the circumstances. At the time, I thought he was crazy and told him so, but I've had some time to think about things since then, and I think he was right to call the wedding off. It would have been a disaster waiting to happen, on both sides."

"You...you're not too upset about it, then?"

She smiled an odd little smile. "Oh, I wouldn't go that far. But I'm a realist, Celia. It's you Luke loves, not me. Believe me, if he hadn't been unconscious when he was brought in here, it would have been you he'd have called to his bedside, not me. I was called by mistake. Apparently, there was this letter on the passenger seat of Luke's car which a policeman at the accident scene picked up. It had my parents' name and address on it. He found their number from directory enquiries and I answered. Once I got here, I gave the hospital administration section the job of finding you, which was impossible to begin with, since I only had your christian name to go by. I had to ring Luke's solicitor at home to come up with a surname, plus your mother's name. I presume you're Celia's mother? Jessica?''

Jessica nodded.

"I thought so. You're very alike. And before you ask, yes, Luke told me everything about you and his dad, too.''

"*Everything?*'' Jessica echoed disbelievingly.

"Pretty well everything,'' Isabel confirmed drily. "To be honest, I didn't know Lionel had it in him. Luke, either, for that matter. It seems the Freeman men can be the very devil when it comes to stunningly beautiful redheads with gorgeous green eyes.''

Celia was astounded by such extravagantly generous compliments from this woman whom she considered far more beautiful than any woman she'd ever seen.

"I—I want you to know, Isabel, that I didn't set out to steal Luke away from you. It just…happened.''

Isabel reached out to pat Celia's arm in yet another generous gesture. "I understand what happened more than you realise. Now, I think I'd best be going. Luke will come round again in due time. That's his bed down in the far corner of the ward. Oh, and don't be too alarmed by his bruises. The doctor said bruises always look worse than they really are.''

"I'm used to bruises,'' Celia remarked and Isabel nodded.

"That's right. You're a physiotherapist, aren't you?''

"Yes.'' Boy, Luke really did tell her everything, didn't he?

"That'll come in handy when he's recuperating. You'll be able to give him lots of lovely massages.''

Celia was taken aback by the wickedly sexy glitter that suddenly sparkled in those beautiful blue eyes. Not Miss Cool at all, she realised. Miss Naughty was more like it. Celia suspected that, despite the ladylike façade Luke's ex-fiancée wore so smoothly, she was probably hot stuff in bed.

Celia's first reaction was jealousy, but only for a split second. Any intimacy this woman had shared with Luke was in the past. He was hers now.

"You will stay with him today and see to his needs?'' Isabel asked.

No sexy innuendo this time. Just sincere caring.

"Of course,'' Celia promised. "And Isabel...''

"Yes?''

"I'm really *very* sorry. You've been incredibly understanding about this. I know you must be still feeling terrible...inside.''

"As I said, not so terrible, now that I've adjusted to the idea. We weren't in love, you know. We were just...compatible. I thought it was enough. Obviously, it wasn't.''

"Being in love is what matters most," Jessica murmured rather wistfully, and Isabel's top lip curled over.

"I can't agree with that," she said. "But everyone's entitled to their opinion. Look, get Luke to ring me when he feels up to it, will you, Celia? He'll know where to find me. He gave me his town house in Sydney as a parting gift. And he's promised me loads of lovely money, so don't go feeling too sorry for me. I'll be fine."

"I'll just bet she will," Jessica muttered once Isabel was out of earshot. "Now, that's one tough cookie, despite her butter-wouldn't-melt-in-her-mouth appearance."

"I don't think she's all that tough," Celia mused. "I think she's just been hurt. Not by Luke. By someone else, in the past…"

"So what's got into you? You used to be the cynical one, not me. But enough of her, let's go and see Luke."

Celia had claimed she wouldn't be alarmed by Luke's bruises, but she *was* alarmed, both by them and the pallor of his skin. Her heart squeezed tight as she stared down at his sleeping form. She wanted to hold him so badly but, of course, that would have been stupid, and painful for a man with broken ribs.

Celia quietly drew the curtain around the bed and both she and Jessica pulled up chairs.

"He looks dreadful," Jessica said, echoing Celia's thoughts.

"I *feel* dreadful." Luke groaned, his eyes opening to slits first, then opening a little further.

Their eyes met and he smiled at her. "You found me," he said.

She picked up his nearest hand with both of hers and pressed it to her cheek. "You silly, silly man," she choked out. "I hope you weren't speeding."

Slowly, carefully, he shook his head.

"That's good." She kissed each of his fingers in turn, and her heart swelled up with such love for him.

"You must have been worried when I didn't turn up last night," he said hoarsely.

She looked into his eyes and smiled. "That's putting it mildly."

"Poor Celia…"

"She was in a dreadful state this morning," her mother piped up. "When the policeman knocked on the door, she collapsed."

"Mum, don't exaggerate. I didn't actually collapse, Luke."

"Close to," her mother muttered.

Luke brought her hand up to his mouth and kissed it. "You will marry me, won't you?" he murmured.

Celia stared at him.

"Now, look here," her mother piped up again. "You've only known each other for a day or so. That's not nearly enough time to make such a big decision as marriage."

Luke smiled at her. "How ironic that *you*, of all people, Jessica, would be the one to give us that advice."

"What do you mean?"

Luke propped himself up on his elbows before grunting painfully then dropping back onto the pillows.

"Look around the bed, Celia," he said, still grimacing. "Can you see my bag anywhere? It's black. A sports bag."

It was under the bed, in the special space made to put the patient's personal things when the bed was wheeled from room to room, which was often in a hospital.

"Here it is." She dragged it out.

"Open it. In it, on top, you should find a couple of sheets of paper folded over."

"Yes, here they are."

"I want you to give them to your mother to read."

Celia raised her eyebrows at her mother as she handed them over.

"I hope that will put your mind at rest, Jessica," Luke said, "in more ways than one."

CHAPTER FOURTEEN

"MY DEAREST Jess," it began.

Jessica looked up, her heart racing.

"Where—where did you find this?" she asked Luke shakily.

"It was in a secret drawer," he told her. "In my father's desk. I found it yesterday. Just read it, Jessica."

Her eyes dropped back to the paper but her hands were trembling. Fear of what she was about to find out gripped her heart like a vice. But nothing short of death could stop her from reading her lover's letter.

How strange it is that in all the years of our relationship, I have never written to you. No, not strange. Sad. Sad and unforgiveable. So much of what I have done to you has been unforgiveable, my darling. God, I regret so much. I should have left Kath as soon as I met you. I knew, that very first night, that you were the right woman for me.

But I was a coward. I couldn't bear the thought of my son hating me as I'd hated my own father. Still, that's no excuse. And now...now it is too late. It would kill Kath if I left her now, so we must continue as we have been.

But I had this dream a couple of nights back, in which

I died suddenly. And it's been bothering me ever since. So yesterday, I organised to give you the deed to our house. I should have done it earlier but, then, you never did like me giving you things. So independent, my lovely Jess. My brave, bold, beautiful Jess.

If only I could go back in time. But of course, you can't. But if I could, I would never let you go, right from that first night. I would be brave and bold too, if I had a second chance. I would not waste a minute of the precious gift of love God blessed us with.

Not many people love as we have loved over the years. With our whole bodies and hearts and minds. We were truly one, my darling, even when we were apart. I thought of you first thing in the morning every morning and last thing at night every night. I find myself writing this as though we're already in the past, I don't know why. That stupid dream, I suppose. But it has left me with an odd feeling of premonition. That is why I am putting my feelings down on paper just in case fate steps in and I don't ever have the chance to hold you in my arms again and tell you how much I love you. Have I told you that often enough, my darling? Have I given you at least some happiness as well as the pain?

I must close this as I have to go out shortly to some ghastly dinner party. I'd much rather be there with you, sitting on our deck, talking and sipping wine together.

Suddenly, I feel so sad. And I'm rambling. I told you about Luke getting married soon, didn't I? You know, I'm still not sure about him and that girl of his. They're too calm around each other. They never argue. Or hug, or kiss. Do you remember how we used to be during those first tempestuous months? Always arguing. Just so we could make up in bed. What passion we shared, my darling. What magic. That kind of magic only comes along once in a lifetime and, for some people, not at all. If only I'd realised that.

But we can't go back, can we? Still, at least I can tell you how much I treasured the times we spent together. Never forget me, Jess, because I'll never forget you, or stop loving you, no matter what. And please, please forgive me. I'm sure we will see each other again soon but, till then, I'll pop this in the mail to you first thing in the morning. Hopefully, the deed of your house shouldn't be long in following.

All my love, my darling,

Lionel.

Jessica touched his signature with her fingertips, silent tears dripping off her nose onto the paper.

Luke had a pretty good idea of what Celia's mother was feeling at that moment. He'd been more than moved when he'd read that letter. And so relieved that his dad had really loved his mistress, but had still cared enough for his wife not to destroy her faith in her husband, the one man whom she must have thought really loved her.

The letter had also galvinised Luke into action. Because no way were he and Celia going to end up like his father and her mother had!

Jessica looked up at him, her lovely eyes flooded. "You're right," she choked out. "Marry her. Soon."

Celia sucked in sharply.

"I will, don't worry," Luke said. "If she'll have me." And he looked at Celia. "Well, darling? Will you marry me?"

She looked a little bewildered but her answer was strong. "Of course I will."

"No hesitation? No doubts?"

"None."

"Incredible."

"There's a coffee shop down in the foyer," Jessica said, sniffling. "I'm going to take myself down there for a while. I'd like to read Lionel's letter again, in private, if you don't mind."

"We don't mind," Luke answered.

"You'll have to tell me what was in that letter," Celia whispered after her mother walked off, "or risk my dying of curiosity."

When Luke told her what was in it, Celia's heart turned over. "Oh, I'm so glad you found that letter," she said. "Poor Mum's been so desolate, thinking your dad didn't really love her."

"I know. I was worried he mightn't have as well. I feel much better knowing that he did."

"Sad, though, that they were never together as they should have been, as man and wife. I know Mum would have dearly loved to have had Lionel's child."

"Which is why we're not going to make the same

mistake, madam,'' Luke said firmly. ''We're going to get married, pronto.''

''How quick is pronto? I want a white wedding with all the trimmings. Mum will want that for me too, since she didn't have one herself.''

Luke groaned. ''What is it with women and weddings? That'll take weeks and weeks.''

''Nothing's stopping us living together as soon as you're well enough to get out of here.''

He smiled. ''Now, why didn't I think of that? Where?''

''Where what?''

''Where shall we live together?''

''Well, I have this nice little flat behind the clinic where I work. It has all the essentials. A fridge. A television. A bed...''

''Sounds perfect.''

''What about your job in Sydney?''

''My contract is up for renewal. I simply won't renew it.''

''Just like that?''

''Just like that.''

Celia grinned. ''I love a decisive man.''

''What about babies?''

Her eyebrows arched. ''What *about* babies?''

''I want more than one.''

''You know, you'll have to learn to ask, Mr Freeman,'' she said with a twinkle in her eye, ''not just tell me.''

''You're right. How many babies do you want?''

"I think four is a nice even number."

"Wow! That's two more than I had in mind."

"Shall we compromise with three?"

"Hell, no, let's be bold and go for four."

"But not during the first year," she replied. "I want you all to myself for a while."

"Tut-tut, you must *ask*, Ms Gilbert, not just tell me."

Celia bit her bottom lip and tried to look chastened. "Could I please have you all to myself for a year, darling?"

"Only on one condition."

"What's that?"

"You go on the pill. No more condoms for me."

"Done."

"How about a little kiss?" he asked softly.

"Luke Freeman, you're supposed to be too sore and sorry for such nonsense."

"Amazing what pethidine can do, isn't it?"

"Well...just a little kiss."

Their mouths touched lightly, sweetly.

"I love you," he murmured when their lips lifted slightly.

"I love you too."

"Put your head down here, beside mine," he said, patting the pillow next to him.

She did, closing her eyes when her nose touched his cheek. This will be what it'll be like, she thought, waking up with him in the mornings.

"I know other people will think we're rushing things," he whispered, "and so did I, till I read that letter my father wrote to your mother. He made me realise how important it was to seize the day because who knows what the future could bring? I decided then and there to come back and make you marry me.''

''*Make* me marry you?''

''*Ask* you to marry me,'' he rephrased.

She smiled. ''That's better, though actually, I rather like it when you're being forceful. Especially in bed.''

''Is that so?''

''Yes, that's so.''

''I'll remember that.''

''Luke…?''

''Yes, my darling?''

''I liked your Isabel.''

''I did too.''

''She wants you to give her a ring sometime.''

''I'll do that. Which reminds me, I gave her the town house I've been living in, and I'm going to organise for her to have an independent income. I hope you don't mind.''

''I don't mind at all. But money isn't everything, is it? I mean…I'd hate to think she's going to be miserable without you.''

''She didn't love me, Celia. She'll survive.''

''That's what she said.''

''And so will your mum.''

''Poor Mum…''

''No, don't think that. She experienced a great love in her life which is something a lot of people are never lucky enough to do.''

"We're even luckier then, aren't we?"

"Yep."

"I hope Isabel finds a great love one day."

"I hope so too."

"You are a very good man, Luke Freeman. You're going to make a very good father."

"I hope so. I had a good example set for me."

"Yes…" Celia nodded slowly. "Yes, as much as I hate to admit it, Lionel was a good father. You know, when I was a little girl I used to fantasise about Lionel being my *real* father."

"Really? That reminds me of something I've been meaning to ask you. Who *was* your real father? Or don't you know?"

"Oh, I know all right. He was just a boy. A classmate of Mum's. They got very merry at an end-of-year party and the result was me. Mum was just sixteen at the time. He was all of seventeen. When she told him she was pregnant, he wanted her to get an abortion. So did his parents. So did *her* parents. But Mum always did have a mind of her own. When her parents wouldn't support her decision to have the baby, she left home and supported herself.

"Gran and Pop came round later after I was born, but I never really knew them well. They died when I was a teenager. I never had anything to do with my real father. He seemed to want it that way. Which was perhaps why I was so vulnerable to your father's attentions. I thought he was wonderful."

"He *was* wonderful."

"If you say so, darling." Privately, Celia still wasn't

so sure about that. But she could afford to be generous, under the circumstances. "Do you know that when we have a baby, Lionel will be his or her grandfather, and my mother will be his or her grandmother. It's almost as if they *were* married, isn't it?"

"What a lovely way of putting it."

"It *was* destiny that we be together, wasn't it? Just like you said."

"Yes, darling, I think it was. Now, give me another little kiss, then why don't you pop downstairs and see how your mum is? Maybe she'll let you read that letter for yourself. I might have left some important things out."

Celia went downstairs to the coffee shop and found her mother sitting at a corner table, looking more serene than she'd seen her in years. Celia didn't have to ask to read the letter, her mum just handed it to her.

"Here," she said, smiling softly. "I want you to read this."

Celia still started reading Lionel's letter with a slightly cynical heart. But, by the time she finished, her eyes were full of tears.

"Oh, Mum," she cried, dabbing at them with a serviette. "Luke was right and I was wrong."

"About what, darling?"

"Lionel *was* wonderful."

"Oh, yes," her mother said, her own green eyes glistening. "Yes, he was."

Celia folded the letter over and handed it back. But not quite as wonderful as his son, she thought. No. Not quite *that* wonderful.

EPILOGUE

LUKE almost jack-knifed up from the massage table.

"Woman!" he complained as he slowly sank back down again. "What happened to the notion of healing hands? If your mother gave massages anything like you do, then my father would have run a mile."

"My mother gives a different type of massage," Celia said drily. "I'm not trying to relax you, I'm trying to make you mobile again."

"I was pretty mobile last night, wasn't I?"

"Oh, phooey. You just lay on your back while I did all the work."

"True." Luke sighed with pleasure at the memory. "Do you think we could try that again? After all, everyone else's gone home. It's just you, me and an empty clinic."

"Not just yet. Now, shut up and endure."

Luke shut up and endured. He'd only been out of the hospital for a week and he knew Celia was only doing what was best for him. But brother, when those amazingly strong fingers of hers had kneaded his right thigh muscle just now, he'd almost gone through the roof.

"Speaking of the clinic," Celia added as she worked on his calf, "Carol gets back from her maternity leave in a couple of weeks and I don't really want to stay on

184

here. It's not my cup of tea. But the flat goes with the job, so we'll have to find somewhere else to live, I'm afraid. Sorry.''

''No need to apologise. What would you think about coming to live in Sydney with me? We could stay at the family home till I sell it.''

''You're still determined to sell it, Luke? From what you've said it's a lovely old place.''

''It is. But I think we should have a place of our own, something we designed and built together.''

''Oh, I'd love that.''

''Up this way.''

She beamed. ''You mean that?''

''I surely do. I can set up shop anywhere. It doesn't have to be in Sydney. So what say during the couple of months we have leading up to our wedding, we buy a parcel of land right on the Lake somewhere? I'll draw up the plans with your approval and submit them to council. Getting a builder will be easy. I know plenty of good builders. Then, they can build our dream home while we have an extended honeymoon overseas. You did say you wanted me all to yourself for a year, didn't you?''

''I certainly did.''

''Then, we'd be killing two birds with one stone, because it'll take a year for me to show you everything. You said you'd never been overseas before.''

''Never.''

''Then, I'll have to take you to London and Paris and

Rome and New York. New York will blow your mind. And then there's Tahiti. Now, *there's* a place for a honeymoon. Yes, we'll start in Tahiti, with nothing to do for a while except swim and lie back in hammocks and make love.''

"Sounds wonderful," Celia said dreamily. "Almost too good to be true."

Luke turned over and looked up into her eyes. "Nothing's too good for you, my darling."

She smiled down at him. "Such sweet talk will get you everywhere."

He cocked an eyebrow at her. "Will it get me a change in massage technique?"

"What did you have in mind?"

He picked up her hands and placed them right on where he had in mind.

"Gently now," he murmured when her hands began to move.

"Like this?"

"Mmm."

"And like this?"

He moaned softly.

She abandoned him for a second to turn and pick up a nearby bottle of fragrant oil. "I think we might need some of this, don't you?"

Luke was in heaven. There again, when Celia was making love to him, he was always in heaven.

"Do with me as you will," he said with a sigh of blissful surrender.

"Oh, I will," she said saucily. "I most certainly will."

Luke closed his eyes and wallowed while the woman he loved most certainly did.

*   *   *   *   *

The Dysarts
A family with a passion for life—and for love.

by *Catherine George*

Get to know the Dysarts!

Over the coming months, you can share the dramas and joys, and hopes and dreams of this wealthy English family, as unexpected passions, births and marriages unfold in their lives.

Look out for...

RESTLESS NIGHTS
Harlequin Presents® #2244
on-sale April 2002

and

SWEET SURRENDER
Harlequin Presents® #2285
on-sale November 2002

The world's bestselling romance series.

Seduction and Passion Guaranteed!

Available wherever Harlequin books are sold.